Preloved

Ira W

ISBN: 978-1-7773780-0-4

I would like to dedicate this book to all my readers. Thank you for your support.

Contents

Chapter 1

Noor

"Thank you so much for agreeing to this marriage, my dear."

My mother placed her hand on my shoulder and kissed my head to reassure me that the step I agreed to take was the right thing to do under current circumstances.

Everything was happening too fast, but my family needed it—his family needed it. This decision was made for the people that I deeply cared about, and I loved my family too much to turn them down when they presented this proposition to me. It hadn't even been a week since the horrific accident happened where I lost my best friend—my older sister, Mariam—and now, here I was waiting in my room so that I could be taken to the man who would become my husband in just a few moments.

"It's time."

My father entered the room and I looked at him. His eyes got teary as soon as he glanced my way and witnessed me in the wedding dress that my mother managed to pull together for me in just two days. I walked toward my father and embraced him. I was missing my sister terribly. I wished she were here with us. If she were here, then none of this would have happened in the first place. This marriage was nothing but a compromise. It was always going to be a compromise.

“Baba,” I managed to utter in a broken voice. Some part of me was still lost somewhere. All the memories that I shared with my lovely sister were wandering inside my head since the day she passed away. I couldn’t let go of it, the pain and sorrow were indescribable. It felt like a part of my soul had gone with her.

“Let’s go.”

He placed his hands around my shoulders to keep me steady as we walked downstairs.

“You’re doing the right thing; Mariam would have wanted this,” my mother whispered, and that made it worse. I wanted to tell her Mariam wasn’t here, and if she were, none of this would have happened, but I kept quiet. The idea of her not being with us was still unacceptable. Destiny was playing a game with me. Never in a million years had I thought that one day I’d be doing this.

The music started playing as we entered the living room.

“Stop the music,” the man spoke, and the music stopped.

I looked up from the ground and saw Ayaan, who was like a friend to me once upon a time—and also my brother-in-law. No, he wasn’t my brother-in-law anymore…he was my future husband. He was dressed in a black suit, hair parted sideways, with a little scruff. He seemed older compared to last time I saw him, when he was here with Mariam…when everything was fine. How quickly did everything change? From so much happiness and celebration to sadness and misery.

“Noor.”

His mother came forward and held my hands to take me

to the sofa where Ayaan was sitting. He stiffened and moved further back as soon as I sat next to him. I duplicated his manner and scooted away from him, too. He noticed, but remained silent.

"Well, everyone is here, Maulvi Sahib," my father announced to the Imam to start the wedding ceremony.

I felt completely numb. I wasn't in a position to think, argue, or react. So I sat there and waited. Ayaan agreed to this marriage with such loath in his voice that every time he said yes, my heart ached.

"And do you take Mohammad Ayaan Khalid as your husband, Ms. Noor Ahmed?" the Imam asked me, and everyone turned to look at me except Ayaan. *I don't think I can do this*, my heart screamed, but my brain didn't allow me to act on it.

"Noor?"

My mom hurried to me and placed her hand on my back, and I couldn't stop myself from crying. *I hope I'm making the right decision*, I tried to tell myself, thinking about the reason that made me say yes to this agreement in the first place, the only reason I accepted to tie my name with Ayaan's.

"Think about Hamza," my mother reminded me, and I thought about my sister's child. My two-month-old nephew who did nothing to deserve this. He needed me. He was the reason I was choosing to become a part of Ayaan's life—so I could raise my sister's child as my own.

"I..." I gulped, and then Ayaan turned his head and stared right into my eyes. That was the first time he had looked at me since the funeral. His eyes were bloodshot. I only saw hatred and loss in them, nothing else. His suffering gaze sent chills down my spine, and I glanced away immediately.

"Noor, do you take Mohammad Ayaan Khalid as your husband?" the Imam asked.

"Yes," I uttered.

"Do you take Mohammad Ayaan Khalid as your husband?" he repeated.

"Yes," I replied and clenched my dress.

"Do you take Mohammad Ayaan Khalid as your husband?" he asked for the very last time.

"Yes." I said, breaking down on my mother's shoulder.

My father's close friends began congratulating him and Ayaan's father—they came to the ceremony to act as witnesses. Ayaan's mother approached me with two gold bangles that once belonged to my sister.

"Aunty," I shook my head to deny accepting them. I couldn't wear these. They belonged to my sister. They weren't mine. They could never be mine. These bangles were given to my sister when she married Ayaan.

"I gave these to Mariam, and now you're the mother of her child. You're Ayaan's wife," she declared, and as soon as she said that, Ayaan got up from the sofa.

"I have to go. I'm sorry, Baba."

He looked at my father, who nodded, allowing him to leave. Ayaan didn't even glance at me as he angrily marched out the door. Could he not see that I lost my sister, too? That I was in pain, too?

My parents drove me to Ayaan's house after all the guests had left. My mother helped me set up the last few things in my new room. Most of my stuff had already been moved and was put in the right place. This new arrangement was nothing compared to my room in my parents' house. Like most things, everything was strange. I was borrowing a part of my sister's life that I shouldn't be.

"Ammi, please stay with me," I pleaded as my mother picked up her bag to leave.

"We'll come tomorrow, my dear. This is your home now."

My mother wiped away the tears from my face.

"Please, stay for a little while."

I grabbed her hand.

"Noor, this family needs you. They're your responsibility now. We'll see you tomorrow."

My father joined us and hugged me. I loved my parents dearly; everything that I was doing was for them and my nephew. They stayed with me with a few more moments but eventually left with a promise of coming to visit me soon.

"Huma will be here if you need anything. Let me show you where some of Hamza's things are kept," Ayaan's mother said, entering the room after I changed into comfortable clothes.

Ayaan's mother—who had been taking care of Ayaan and Hamza since Mariam's funeral—was running off to a business meeting, but she was making sure I got settled before she left. His father hadn't stuck around. I didn't know too much about the situation, but I knew Ayaan's parents were separated—Mariam had mentioned that

Ayaan and his father weren't close.

His mother was referring to Huma, the housekeeper, who was a kind and simple middle-aged woman that I knew quite well because Mariam was very fond of her.

"Thank you so much, my dear, for agreeing to this marriage. Hamza and Ayaan both need you…I am indebted to you," she said as the tour of the house concluded.

"Please don't say that…I just did what felt right…for Hamza."

I smiled at her and walked with her to the door. Hamza was staying at my parents' because they wanted me to spend some time alone with Ayaan so we could talk some things out. I hated that idea, but they insisted. What was I supposed to say to him?

I stayed awake and decided to wait for Ayaan in the living room, but he didn't show up. I went to his room—our room, I corrected myself. It felt so weird to suddenly have his name tied to mine.

Everywhere I looked, I saw pictures of Mariam and Ayaan, both looking happy and absolutely in love. It brought tears to my eyes. Mariam was so young. She was perfect. Why did such a thing happen to her? Why did bad things happen to good people?

I stepped closer to the pictures and grabbed one of the frames. This frame had a picture from their wedding day. I was also in it, sitting between them. Ayaan and Mariam had their arms around me, and I was smiling big for the camera. We all seemed so happy.

Nothing will ever be the same.

"What are you doing in here?"

The voice came from behind and I jumped, dropping the photo frame on the floor, smashing it to pieces.

Ayaan was here.

Chapter 2

Noor

The room felt a lot smaller when Ayaan walked over to me and stared down at the broken frame. I got on my knees to pick up the glass pieces. He didn't say a word, just watched.

"Noor," he finally spoke, and I looked at him. "Get up," he ordered, and I did just that. I held onto the picture.

"You can sleep downstairs in the guest room." He turned around and headed to the dressing table.

"Okay," I nodded and was about to walk out the door when he said my name again and I stopped.

"I want to make a few things clear. Although we are married, I'll never consider you my wife. You are only here for Hamza, and you don't have to look after me. If you need anything, tell Huma and she'll take care of it." He sounded like a robot. He showed no emotion when he said those words to me. Why didn't he realize that he wasn't the only one who lost her? Mariam meant everything to me, too. I lost her, too. I was suffering, too.

"I understand. I will keep out of your way, but I only have one request. My parents have gone through a lot, and I don't want them to worry about me. So, whenever you see them, please assure them that everything's fine between us," I asked him. My parents had so many hopes for me. I didn't want them to feel disappointed or guilty for putting me in such a situation.

He didn't respond to my request and went to the washroom. I walked downstairs and saw Huma cleaning around the living room area.

"Do you need any help?" I asked her. I knew I wouldn't get myself to sleep. I'd be wide awake with the same tiring thoughts that were running through my head all the time.

"No, I'm almost done, dear. You should go and rest," she replied gently.

"I can't sleep," I told her honestly.

"Should I make you some tea?" she offered, and I nodded. Tea was my weakness. We made our way to the kitchen and she started making some for me.

"Mariam also loved tea. She used to tell me to make tea for her many times a day."

Huma poured tea into a beautiful gray and gold designed cup with an M on it and handed it to me.

"Yes, she did." I smiled, thinking about the times I spent with my sister where we would talk for hours and hours, having numerous cups of tea and watching our favorite films and television shows.

"Do you have a family?" I didn't know much about Huma's personal life. She was probably in her early fifties.

"This is my family...I met Ayaan when he was about eleven years old or so, and I've been taking care of him ever since." She cared about him so much. She spoke of him with so much love in her voice. She spent almost twenty-two years here, taking care of Ayaan. That was such a long time.

"You didn't get married?"

"I was married once; my husband was a police officer. We eloped because I was from a different caste. Months after our marriage, I got a call from the police force and they told me he got shot during the political clash. So I started working at people's houses to clean and cook food for them because I couldn't go back to the village. Then, one day, I met Ayaan's mother and she asked me to look after him full-time. I've been here ever since."

"I'm sorry about your loss Huma." I felt bad about how she must have felt when she received that call about her husband's death. I tried to find the right words, but the truth was no matter how hard you try to recognize and feel someone's pain, you can't. You cannot know pain unless you're the one going through it. The pain I was feeling after losing one of the greatest people in my life was true evidence of that.

"It was a long time ago... Anyway, do you need anything else?" she asked me. I wanted her to sit and talk to me, but I could tell she was sleepy. The past few days would have been hard for her, as well, dealing with Ayaan's moods.

"No, you should go and get some sleep. Thank you for the tea," I told her. She went to her room, located on the other side of the property, separated by a huge lawn.

Since I couldn't sleep, I grabbed a book from the library and took my tea to the living room. I quietly turned on the television and opened the book, a memoir about a woman during the time of war and how she coped up with the loss of her parents, remaining strong to look after her younger siblings. My sister designed the library in this house and all the books here were chosen by her. She decorated everything, picking every painting and piece of furniture to match her style. This house was her haven. I was just praying to find my place in it.

I kept reading until my eyes started aching and I closed them, at last, allowing the heavy night to take over.

Chapter 3

Noor

Next morning when I woke up I noticed that there was a blanket covering me. Did Ayaan cover me up yesterday? No, he would never do that. It was probably Huma.

"*Assalam O Alaikum,*" Huma greeted me warmly as she entered the living room with my clothes that were nicely pressed, placing them in front of me.

"Walikum Asalam. What time is it?" I asked her and went through the clothes, picking a blue and green colored dress to change into.

"It's eight. What would you like for breakfast?" Huma asked me.

"Prepare whatever Ayaan likes," I simply told her. I didn't want to change or do anything to cause any disruption in his house.

"Thanks for the blanket," I mentioned to her as I was leaving to go to the washroom.

"I didn't bring the blanket, dear." She smiled at me and left for the kitchen. So Ayaan *was* the one who did it.

I took a quick shower and changed into fresh clothes, which helped me look somewhat presentable. When I entered the kitchen, I saw Ayaan dressed in a white collared shirt and gray pants, sleeves folded as usual. His eyes were still red and heavy. Was he crying last night? I wouldn't dare ask. I took a seat as far away from him as possible and kept my eyes down. Huma was still preparing breakfast.

"Did you sleep well?" Ayaan asked me from the other side of the table, and I looked at him. There was so much I wanted to say to him, but couldn't.

"Yes." I nodded and got up from my seat to help Huma with the preparation. I hated the silence between us. We were never this quiet with each other before.

After breakfast was ready, I took the plate with a cheese omelet and naan bread to him, along with a cup of tea, and placed it in front of him. I went back to my seat and started eating in silence. Huma excused herself to talk to the gardener outside.

"I was thinking...I think we should go and get Hamza," I told him. I hated being alone.

"Hmm," he responded. Since the funeral, he hadn't even held Hamza in his arms, not even once.

"He needs you." I reminded him of his responsibility toward his son. He should be mindful of his duties.

"I'm aware of my duties. You don't have to tell me what to do," he said harshly and picked up a newspaper to escape the conversation.

"I know you don't need anyone, especially not me. But he's your son, he needs you." I kept my voice low.

"Fine. If you care about him so much, then from now on you take care of him."

How could he be so bitter toward his own child?

"Ayaan, please, don't behave like this; I'm only trying to help you. Believe me, I only want what's best for this family...and I know it's been very difficult..." Why was I even justifying myself? I was in a terrible position.

"Who gave you this right? Who asked for your help?" He threw his plate across the floor and left the room. I debated whether to follow him or not, but I didn't care at this point, so I ran after him.

"You can't just walk away every time," I shouted at him when I entered his room.

"I can do whatever I want," he replied rudely.

"Why are you like this, Ayaan? Hamza is your son. He is proof of your love for Mariam." Tears filled my eyes.

"Mariam isn't here, Noor," he shouted back, loud enough for me step back in fear.

"So you're just going to be like this forever? You're not going to look after your son? You're not going to talk about your feelings? You're going to suffer and give everyone else a hard time, too?" I yelled, looking at him with disappointment. He turned around to face me, and the way he looked at me, I thought he was going to eat me alive. But he didn't say a word.

"Tell me, why are you so quiet now? Answer me. Are you going to be like this and act like you don't care?" I stepped forward and grabbed his collar as I tried my hardest not to cry in front of him. "It's not only you who lost her; I lost her, too. How can you be so selfish?" I demanded. I wanted him to tell me what was going on in his mind. I couldn't figure him out.

Suddenly, Ayaan grabbed both of my wrists and pulled

me closer to him.

"Why are you complaining, huh? I didn't ask to marry you. I didn't ask for you to take care of Hamza. I don't owe you anything." He glared furiously at me. "In fact, I think you should be rather happy. You're living in a big house; you have a servant. You don't have to worry about working to support your family. You should be thankful." He gawked at me.

Yes, our family was middle class and we weren't as rich as Ayaan's family. Yes, I used to work to support my family, and I loved my job. Ayaan knew Mariam was from a middle-class family when he married her, so why was he taunting me about it? He must have been saying it just to get back at me, to make me feel bad. I knew his intentions were not to degrade me, but to make me stop questioning him.

"That wasn't the answer to my question," I challenged him. He thought he'd break me, but sadly for him, that was not so easy. It wasn't easy to break something that was already broken. Yes, I was sensitive and I cared, but that didn't make me weak. He was the weak one, because he was in denial.

He pushed me away and left the room. Minutes later, I heard him telling Huma that he was going out and he'd be back late. This confirmed that there was no place for me in this house. I picked up my bag and asked the driver to drop me at my parents' house so I could see Hamza, who was my responsibility now. I was going to take care of him.

Chapter 4

Noor

After finishing lunch with my family, we all finally sat together and a strange silence fell upon us. Baba was quiet and waited for my mother to speak, but she remained soundless as well. Hamza was sleeping deeply in my arms. I hadn't left his side since I arrived at my parents' house, and he held onto my finger with his small hand as if he was afraid to let go, thinking I might disappear just like his parents. I finally felt some peace in my heart when I glanced at his sleepy face and saw him resting calmly; he was loved—love he should have been getting from his own father, who was nowhere in sight.

"We think you should go back home, dear," my mother spoke at last, and I looked up at her. She and Ayaan were always close; she considered him her own son and perhaps couldn't see his faults.

"Ammi, I can't...I can't stay there...it's too hard. Ayaan doesn't talk to me. He doesn't even care about his own child...when was the last time he came over to see Hamza since Mariam passed away?" I asked them.

"Noor, things have changed since then, don't you think?" Baba walked over from his chair and sat next to me.

"It's his way of thinking that bothers me, Baba. I don't need Ayaan to take care of me, but why is he punishing himself and Hamza like this? It hurts me," I tried to explain.

"We all had each other when we lost Mariam, but Ayaan...think about it. Did he have anyone by his side? You know how his relationship is with his parents. Mariam was very important to him. Don't you remember when we first met him, he came to our house asking for Mariam's hand in marriage by himself? His parents weren't a part of it. Noor, men react to pain differently than women do; women are tougher, they have more strength to fight the pain. For men, however, it's a lot harder."

My father was a philosopher and a family counselor by profession.

"Those are your counselor instincts that are talking right now, Baba," I said with sarcasm.

"No, that's my love for you that's talking. I'm only trying to make you understand a different point of view. Ayaan is not a difficult man, Noor, he's just going through a difficult time." My father smiled and patted my head as if he was already seeing something that I couldn't recognize right now. He seemed satisfied with his advice.

"It's simply a matter of time, Noor. Ayaan will change for better." My mother tried to comfort me.

"He doesn't see anything good in me, Mama. He looks at me as if I am a burden to him," I complained.

"Don't worry, my child, he will see good in you. You know why we named you Noor? Because when I saw you for the first time, I felt that there wouldn't be any more darkness in our lives, and we were right. You always made us proud, just like your sister."

My father had so much confidence in me, and that made me feel even worse. What if I wasn't capable of living up to his expectations?

"He only sees darkness in me, Baba. He only sees me with hate," I told them.

"That's his problem, Noor—it has nothing to do with you. Even if he only sees darkness in you, it doesn't mean he's right. You will always bring light, Noor; it's part of you." My father once again answered my concerns with optimism.

"I'm afraid I won't be able to light his life, Baba." I managed to smile regardless.

Baba dropped me and Hamza off at Ayaan's house before supper. Huma helped me move all the stuff out of the car, and after saying goodbye to Baba, I finally stepped inside the house with Hamza in my arms.

"I have made fried rice today. Go and wash up, and I'll serve dinner." Huma took Hamza from me.

"Okay...where's Ayaan?" I asked her, hoping she'd tell me that he'd asked about me.

"He came in the afternoon and then left again," she reported.

"Did he ask about me?" I inquired with wishful thinking.

She shook her head and left. What was I thinking? Of course he didn't care.

After dinner, I went to the backyard and asked Huma to join me. All the work was done around the house, Hamza was finally asleep inside, and yet again there was no sign of Ayaan.

A short while later, I heard the front door open and I knew he was finally home. And just then, Hamza started crying. Huma was about to go get him, but I stopped her.

“But he is crying.” Huma looked worried.

“I know, just wait,” I told her, and she sat down again. I heard Ayaan calling out Huma’s name a few times, but he didn’t call out my name at all. That’s how much he despised me. Hamza’s cry went on for another couple of minutes and when it stopped, I looked over at Huma.

“You did that on purpose so Ayaan would go and take care of Hamza?” Huma asked with amusement.

I nodded. I knew Ayaan had a fatherly instinct like my own father. I knew Ayaan wouldn’t be able to ignore his crying child for that long. I asked Huma to go to her room, and I went inside to see Hamza.

When I got to Ayaan’s bedroom, Hamza was already asleep again, but Ayaan wasn’t there. I was about to turn to leave, but when I peeked outside, I spotted him standing out on the balcony, looking at the dark sky.

I debated whether to go outside or not, but before I could make up my mind, Ayaan turned around and his eyes met mine. Without thinking twice, I ran downstairs.

“Why did you come back?” I heard Ayaan’s voice coming from behind me, and I stopped. He walked down to catch up with me. His voice was a lot calmer this time.

“This is my home now, I can come and go whenever I like. But if you want me to leave, please tell me and I’ll go.” I wasn’t scared of him anymore. After speaking with my father, I felt a strange sense of self assurance. His encouraging words made me hopeful and allowed me to not let my emotions get the worst of me. If Ayaan was not willing to compromise, then I had to be the one to show some maturity.

He stayed quiet. Did that mean he didn't want me to go?

I was about to keep heading down the stairs when he called out my name again.

"Don't sleep in the living room this time. I've set up a television for you in your room," he said, and I studied him with shock.

"What?" he asked, pulling his eyebrows together.

"You're not mad?" I watched him.

"About what?" He crossed his arms and took a step forward, invading my space.

"For my leaving...and for coming back with Hamza when you told me you didn't want to see him." I stammered for some reason; I wasn't used to having him this close to me.

He shook his head to say no, but didn't say a word.

"Do you want me to take Hamza downstairs with me?" I asked him.

"No, I'll call you if I need anything," he replied gently and started walking upstairs to his room, stopping midway.

"I'm sorry about what happened in the kitchen this morning."

Ayaan didn't look at me when he said it, but he did apologize. Was Baba right all along? Was I capable of bringing light into Ayaan's life?

Chapter 5

Noor

"My friends will be coming over with their families for dinner tonight," Ayaan informed me as he sat across from me and began eating his breakfast.

"Okay."

I didn't know any of his friends.

"They found out about our marriage and they invited themselves," he said with irritation.

"No, it's fine. I am glad they're coming." I didn't want to give him any wrong impression.

"See you." He picked his bag up and left for the office.

I spent the entire day cleaning the house, ordering fresh flowers, and helping Huma with the cooking while we took turns looking after Hamza.

It was fascinating to see him react to new things. Hamza's so precious to me that any time he did something new, I captured it on my phone as a keepsake.

"You sure you're going to be okay? I can look after him," I told Huma, who took Hamza from me around the time the guests were expected to arrive.

"You go and get ready; the guests will be here soon. I'll take care of him." She tickled Hamza's neck and he giggled in response. He loved spending time with Huma. They were developing such a special bond—it was so wonderful to see.

I went to my room, took a shower, and changed into a beautiful yellow dress my mother got me last year on my birthday. I curled my hair and put on some simple silver earrings to complete the look.

"Oh, you look so beautiful, Noor." Huma took some kohl from her eyes and placed it behind my ear to protect me from an evil eye. My late grandmother used to do the same thing. I was not a superstitious person, but I never stopped her from doing it.

The doorbell rang just then, and I went to open the door. As soon as Ayaan saw me, he stopped at the doorway. The way he set his eyes on me made me feel weird.

"Do I look okay? Should I go change?" I stared back at him, taking a step back. Was I overdressed? I gazed down at my dress.

"No, you look..." He coughed.

His friends came in, so he didn't complete his thought.

"I'm Arfa. I'm Zahir's wife," Arfa introduced them. They were newlyweds and seemed so happy together—the spark in their eyes reflected that, as did the way they looked at each other.

They reminded me Mariam and Ayaan. They used to look at each other like the whole world was theirs and they were made for one another. Watching two people in love can be beautiful or painful depending on one's situation. Despite not wanting to feel that way, I felt the latter. I felt lonely.

"I think Rizwan is here," Ayaan announced a few minutes later when the doorbell rang, and he went to get the door.

"This is Rizwan, his wife, Zehrish, and their son, Umair." Ayaan walked them inside and we greeted each other.

"Sorry to bother you like this, but Zehrish really wanted to meet you...she was very fond of Mariam," Rizwan said to me, but then a look of regret took over his face when his wife glared at him. I knew he didn't want to sound insensitive, so I didn't make any comment to address it.

"Oh, not at all, it's great that you all came by. Dinner is almost ready," I quickly responded to ease him.

Both of the ladies, Zehrish and Arfa, turned out to be really friendly. We talked about families, places to visit, and social gatherings, while the boys got busy talking about politics, sports, and business.

"I'll be right back," I excused myself and went over to the kitchen to check if the food was ready. Ayaan followed me inside.

"Do you need something?" I asked him.

"Yeah. I…you…" he struggled, as if he forgot why he was even here.

"Do you need something?" I asked him again.

"No… it's just…your back." He pointed his finger toward me.

"What?" I stared at him puzzlingly. What was he talking about?

"The zip on your dress is coming loose," he informed me as his eyes met mine.

"Oh." I tried to reach the zipper, but couldn't. I thought it was perfectly fine when I put it on earlier.

He waited for me, but when he noticed me struggling, he walked toward me and placed both of his hands behind my neck. I didn't know how to react, so I stood still.

He fixed the zip of the dress and secured it tightly, his eyes stayed on me the entire time. I glanced away to avoid his gaze.

"Here," he said and took a few steps away from me, crossing his arms against his chest.

"Thank you." I felt my face getting warmer, so I turned around before he could notice and began placing the food out on the table. I shouldn't be feeling this way, I warned myself. The way my heart started pounding when he got closer to me concerned me.

"The mango dessert is amazing, Noor," Rizwan complimented me at the end of the meal.

Everyone praised the food, even little Umair, but Ayaan didn't say anything—though I could tell he liked it. Even the food can get an emotional reaction from him.

"You're a lucky man, Ayaan," Zahir said, and Ayaan gave him a polite little nod.

"We had such a good time, thank you for having us. It was so nice to meet all of you, and Hamza is such a sweet baby. Now you'll have to come visit us at our home," Arfa said to me as I walked her and her husband to the door a little later in the evening.

"Thank you for coming. We will definitely come over," I replied, knowing that it was probably a lie—Ayaan would never take me to his friends' houses.

After we said our goodbyes to both couples, Hamza was asleep, so I took him into my room and started cleaning up.

“Huma will do it.” I didn’t hear Ayaan entering the kitchen.

“She’s had a long day. It’s fine, I’m almost done.” I went to pick up the remaining glasses and somehow hit the corner of the table. Glassware fell to the ground, shattering everywhere. Pain hit my leg instantly. Why did I have to be so clumsy and paranoid around him?

I got on my knees to pick up the glasses, but Ayaan stopped me and pulled me up.

“Are you crazy? The glass is going to cut you.” He gawked at me as if I had lost my mind.

“I won’t cut myself.” I tried to break free from his grip, but he didn’t let go.

“Go and sleep, we’ll clean it up tomorrow,” he said to me. Why was he being so insistent?

“Ayaan, please, go to sleep. I’m almost done.” I hated arguing over silly things, but he had other plans. I pulled my hands away from his and walked to the other side of the table, away from him. “Why are you even here? Shouldn’t you be watching the news or doing some work?” I fired back.

“This is my house; I can do whatever I want,” I heard him say. His arrogance had no limits.

“You’re right, but this is my house, too. That means I can do whatever I want to do, and you can’t stop me.” I glared at him.

"That's it!" In an instant, he walked around the table and grabbed my hand.

"Why do you keep grabbing my hand like that? Let me go!" I protested. He was so maddening.

"You need to shut up right now." Before I could resist, he picked me up and took me to his room.

Chapter 6

Noor

"I'm fine," I kept saying, but Ayaan paid no attention to my words. He put me down on his bed and left the room, returning a few minutes later with an ice pack.

"Ayaan, I'm fine. It's nothing." I held my leg, but he pushed away my hands and sat down in front of him, placing my leg on his lap.

"Let me have a look." He touched my leg to find where I got hurt and reached to fold up my trousers. He watched me as if he was asking for my permission.

I nodded my head, and he gently pressed the ice pack on the bruise.

"Ouch." I reacted when the cold sensation touched my skin.

"Hold still," he responded calmly. Once he was finished, he started to put things away and I took that as a sign for me to leave. Hamza was all alone, anyway.

"Where are you going?" I heard Ayaan from behind when I reached the door.

"To my room. Hamza is alone downstairs." I tried to leave again when Ayaan marched forward and lifted me into his arms one more time.

"Ayaan," I squealed, and I swear I saw him smile slightly

before it disappeared.

"The bruise is going to get worse if you put too much pressure on it." He sounded annoyed, so I didn't say anything.

We entered my room, and I saw Hamza still asleep on my bed. I smiled at him and touched his soft cheeks. Ayaan looked at me strangely.

"What?" I whispered so I didn't wake Hamza up. Instead of saying anything, Ayaan turned his back and left the room. He was being so bizarre.

It took me a while, but I finally found some peace that night. I felt as though some stability might be possible—we might all be able to move ahead with our lives.

The next morning was a cold one. I put extra layers on Hamza so he didn't catch a cold and a wore thick sweater to keep myself warm.

"Assalam O Alaikum," I addressed Huma, who was preparing for breakfast.

I joined her in the kitchen, and we began our day with a cup of tea. I waited for Ayaan to come downstairs, but he didn't. It was so unlike him; he was usually an early riser. I knocked on his door, but there was no answer, so I gently opened the door and saw him shivering in his sleep. His body was as hot as hell and he was sweating. He probably didn't turn the heater on in his room and caught a cold.

I walked out of the room to call for Huma and she came up running.

I kept saying Ayaan's name, but he didn't react.

I hurried Huma to call the doctor and some time later he showed up and gave Ayaan an injection. He moved a little in response a few moments later, and I finally took a breath of relief.

"What happened to him? Why was he sweating and cold?" I asked the doctor when I walked him to the door.

"Ayaan is not taking his medication, and it happens when you…" he started.

"What medication?" I interrupted. I didn't know Ayaan took any medication, and Huma never mentioned it.

"He has diabetes. Don't you know?" He presumed, probably wondering how a wife didn't know her own husband's health conditions.

"What?" My sister never mentioned this to me—or maybe I never paid attention.

"Make sure he takes his medication on time." The doctor said as he left, and I went back to the room to look after Ayaan. He was finally awake.

"Hey." I sat beside him and touched his forehead. He pulled away from my touch, but I extended my arm further and pushed him back onto the pillow.

"Let me check. It's going to get worse if you move too much," I repeated his words from last night, and he rolled his eyes.

"Stay here. I called your assistant to let him know you won't be coming to work today." He was about to say something—something rude, probably—so I put my finger on his lips. He looked at me as if I had surprised him, so I pulled my hand away.

I went downstairs to make some homemade soup and took it back to his room. Ayaan was sitting up and had Hamza in his arms.

“Here.” I brought the spoon to his lips, and this time he didn’t argue and let me feed him while he played with Hamza. I couldn’t help but smile.

“What’s so funny?” he asked, and I stopped smiling.

“You act like a child sometimes,” I said without thinking.

“Excuse me?” He was taken aback by my comment.

“What?” I pretended as if I didn’t know what he was talking about.

I was about to feed him another spoonful, but he stopped me and pushed my hand away. He was so hot and cold all the time. I didn’t argue and asked Huma to take the food away.

“You should try to rest,” I told him as I got up to leave.

“I’m going to work.” He was about to get up, but I went and gently pushed him back on the bed. “You think I’m going to listen to you?” he challenged. There he was, like a child again. So stubborn.

“Look, if you don’t listen to me, I’ll call Aunty and tell her that you’re being difficult.”

I knew Ayaan wouldn’t want me to call his mother, afraid that she’d get worried for no reason. He glared at me, but slowly pulled his legs up on the bed and laid down. Even though he was not that close to his mother, he respected and cared about her. He spent most of his time away from home, so he never got a chance to establish a close relationship with his family.

I picked the blanket up to put on him, but he pushed it down. I stared at him and this time, before he could push the blanket down again, I grabbed his hand and rested it on his side.

"Call me if you need anything," I said at last and went downstairs so he could get some rest.

"How is he?" Huma was dusting the bookshelves when I came downstairs.

"Better," I told her with a sense of ease.

"You were worried about him," she pointed out.

"I would have been worried if it were someone else, too," I automatically replied, realizing I might have sounded defensive.

"I never said anything about that; you don't have to justify yourself." She smiled at me.

"What do you mean?" I asked, taking a step closer to her.

"No one gets worried like that for just anyone, Noor. That was something else." Before I could clear things up with her, she left the room, leaving me alone with my feelings.

Would I have reacted the same way if it was anyone else, or was I more worried because it was Ayaan? No, I stopped my mind from imagining baseless things. I erased even the slightest doubt I had about my feelings toward Ayaan. Ayaan was once my sister's husband and is now nothing but the father of my sister's child. That's all there was to it and it would never change—I wouldn't allow it.

Chapter 7

Noor

"You should go check on Ayaan." Huma entered my room just as I finished feeding Hamza.

"Okay, can you look after Hamza?" I passed him over to Huma and went to Ayaan's room. It was late in the evening, so I wanted him to take his medication.

I knocked on his door but he didn't reply, so I walked inside and saw him sleeping. I touched his forehead. It wasn't hot as before; his temperature was starting to come down. I didn't know if it was intentional, but Ayaan smiled in his sleep and pulled me close, enough that I was lying on top of him.

"Ayaan." I shook his shoulders, but he nuzzled into my neck instead.

I said his name again, louder this time, and he opened his eyes. His hands were still on me, and we looked at each other. I had never been so close to a man before, that's probably why my heartbeat got faster—I mean, there was no way I could feel anything for him. I glanced away as he lifted his hands away from my waist, and I pushed myself away from the bed.

"Sorry." I didn't know why I apologized; he was the one who pulled me toward him.

"Why are you here?" he fired at me.

“It’s time for you to take your medicine.” I opened the drawer and pulled out the tablets for him to take.

“I can do it myself.” He snatched the pills from my hands and started looking for water. I rolled my eyes and brought him a water bottle. That, too, he snatched.

“You can go now.” He ogled me as if I were the last person he ever wanted to see.

“First, you take your medicine, then I’ll go.” I smiled at him on purpose. He growled but finally swallowed the pills. Satisfied, I went to the kitchen and brought up a bowl of soup for him to eat.

“I’m not hungry,” he said right away, getting up from his bed. If he was going to stubborn then so was I. I grabbed his arm to stop him from leaving.

“Why don’t you let me help you?” I asked him, but he didn’t respond right away.

“Why do you want to help me?” he spoke at last, and scowled at me.

“Because I...” *Because I care about you*, I wanted to shout at him. *Because seeing you punish yourself is hurting me.* Wait, what? No. That wasn’t right. I wanted to help him because he was my sister’s husband once, and I considered him a part of the family.

“Because you’re Mariam’s...” Before I could complete my thought, he grabbed my hand—the one I was holding his arm with—and twisted it behind my back. The pain hit me like nothing else, and in response I grabbed his shoulder tightly with my free hand.

“Don’t bring her into this conversation...this is between you and me. Why are you trying to help me now? I understand you're here for Hamza, but you needn't concern yourself about me." He tightened his grip around me, and I pressed my nails harder into his skin, hoping that he would let go. Nothing worked on him.

"Do you feel something for me?" He looked down at me and my eyes went wide.

I hesitated, "...no."

"Then why do I find you secretly staring at me when I'm not looking at you? Why do you ask about me and look after me?" His face got closer with each question.

"Ayaan..." I must be brave. I couldn't steal my sister's love; I couldn't take her place.

"Answer me." His head touched mine, and he closed his eyes.

I couldn't do this. As soon as his hands relaxed a little, I pushed him and he fell, stunned, back on the bed.

"I look after you because it's my duty. I only married you because of Hamza; otherwise I would've left you alone," I said with anger, hating every word that was coming out of my mouth.

I was breathing hard. Ayaan covered the side of his head with his hand, blinking a couple of times, looking rather confused. Then his head fell back, and he started snoring.

I watched him for a second, then slowly walked toward him, only to find him fully asleep. I picked up his medicine from the side table and read the back of the label:

Side Effects: Anxiety, Disorientation, Dizziness, and Hallucinations.

I watched Ayaan again. Maybe he was acting so weird

when he woke up because he took extra doses of the medicine. But what might happen when he wakes up again? I shot another look his way and ran downstairs to my room.

Chapter 8

Noor

I stayed in my room for the rest of the day so I could avoid running into Ayaan. Huma informed me that he was awake and wanted to see Hamza, so I gave him to Huma and told her to give him to Ayaan. The longer I could stay away from him, the better.

"He wants tea." Huma walked into my room as I was putting my washed clothes away in the closet.

"Can you please make it?" I asked her. I didn't want her to do the work, that wasn't my intention. I only wanted to avoid contact with Ayaan. His words from our previous conversation were still echoing in my ears.

"He asked for you to make it," she replied. Confused, I didn't argue. On my way to the kitchen, I saw Ayaan playing with Hamza. Our eyes connected for a second, but I looked away immediately. I made the tea as fast as I could, then called for Huma to take the cup to him.

"You're okay?" she asked me as I handed her the tea.

"Yes, I'm fine." I smiled widely—maybe too widely.

She didn't believe me, but she didn't push the subject either, and I walked out of the kitchen.

"Noor," Ayaan called out as I walked past him, and I stopped. He handed Hamza over to Huma and she took him upstairs as Ayaan walked over to me. I couldn't look him in the eye, so I kept looking down.

"How's your leg?" he asked, and I shot him a look of disbelief. Since when did he care about my pain?

"I asked how your leg was." His voice was louder this time. Maybe the medicine was wearing off.

"Better," I told him, and he nodded. Was that it? That's all he wanted to say? I waited for him to say something else, but he didn't continue, so I turned to leave.

"Noor," he called out again, and I looked over at him.

"What?" I asked in a slightly irritated tone so he would leave me alone.

"Don't talk to me like that," he voiced flatly.

"If you don't like the way I speak, then maybe you shouldn't talk to me." That's it, that'll do it. I wanted him to stay away from me. This attachment that I was feeling toward him was wrong. I knew he would never see me as more than his dead wife's sister, and that I would end up getting hurt. I wanted to protect myself. This was becoming too complicated.

"Great. I won't have to hear your horrible voice." He glared at me as though looks could kill.

"Good. It's settled then." This time, he didn't try to stop me when I walked away from him, and I didn't look back, either. Not even when he threw away his cup of tea.

When I entered the kitchen next morning, Ayaan was already there, but he didn't acknowledge me at all. I wanted this; I wanted him to stay cruel and impolite toward me so I could hate him, but it wasn't working. I was betraying myself.

"Paratha!" I almost squealed when Huma placed a plate of warm potato-filled flatbread in front of me. Food was my weakness. Whenever I felt bad, I always relied on food to make me feel better. I was so busy eating that I didn't even acknowledge Ayaan staring at me with a strange expression, but when I finally did, it was hard for me to look away.

I glared back at him and ripped the flatbread in half, sending him a silent warning. He smashed his newspaper down and walked away.

"What's going on between the two of you?" Huma sat beside me, and I pretended as if I had no clue what she was talking about.

"Don't think you can fool me. Now, tell me what it is...you're behaving strangely these days." She ran her fingers through my hair.

"I don't even know, myself. I don't trust myself around Ayaan." That's all I said.

"Why is that? You knew him before you got married." She didn't get it.

"He was my brother-in-law then; he's my husband now," I stated the obvious.

"What kind of a man did you want to marry, Noor?" She was talking kind of like my father, asking me open-ended question to get me to talk about my emotions.

"Every girl wants a guy who will love her with all his heart. I wanted the same, but I'll never get that kind of love..." I replied to her not-so-simple question. Maybe love wasn't my destiny.

"Let me tell you something: Women tend to fall in love faster than men. Men, however, need time, because even though they look tough, they are just as sensitive as us—the only difference is that they hide their emotions from the world. Whatever happened, leave that behind and try to start fresh. It will be hard for both of you, but I'm sure you'll accept each other at some point. You married Ayaan for the sake of your parents and to look after Hamza, but have you ever thought about why Ayaan married you? He must have noticed something in you—love, maybe—and certainly the love and affection that you have for his child. He trusts you, Noor, and you know what people say: Always trust before you love, because love is baseless without trust." I teared up, and Huma squeezed my hand reassuringly. I hugged her tightly.

A moment later, Ayaan walked into the kitchen, and I parted from Huma and wiped away the tears. He noticed me, but remained silent, though I swore I saw some concern on his face.

"You are leaving for the office?" Huma asked him.

"Yes...I'll be late today. Don't wait for me for dinner." He watched me as he spoke, even though he was facing Huma. When he left, I relaxed in my seat. It started raining outside, and I allowed the sound of it to unwind me.

Chapter 9

Noor

“It’s two in the morning, Noor, you should go sleep.” Huma was sitting on the chair when I entered the living room after putting Hamza to bed after he woke up crying.

“I’m not tired.” I sat beside her.

“Sometimes you remind me so much of Mariam,” Huma said to me. Whenever she talked about Mariam, there was so much admiration and love in her voice for her. I could tell she missed her, too.

“No, she was way better than I am. She was more hardworking, loving, kind...just an overall better person than I will ever be. I’m only trying to be even the slightest bit like her.” I looked at her.

“You’ll never be happy if you keep comparing yourself to Mariam. You’re a different person. You resemble her, yes, but you are you, and she was she; that doesn’t make you a less of a good person than she was.” She patted her lap, and I laid my head down as she started to comb my hair gently with her fingers. She was the reason I didn’t miss my parents that much; having her around felt like having my own parents nearby.

We talked for a few more minutes, then I heard Huma yawn and I got up from her lap.

"You should go sleep." She listened to me and headed to her room.

Just then, the door creaked open, and I went to make sure it was Ayaan. Sure enough, he was finally home. I had wondered where he was.

Even with his full-grown beard and dark bags under eyes from lack of sleep, he still looked good. I couldn't help myself from staring at him. There was no denying that he was blessed with great looks, but these days he seemed different, stressed, and not like his usual self. It was like he wasn't even trying to get better.

He walked right by me, and I followed him.

"Did you eat anything?" I asked him as he took off this coat and loosened his tie. He remained silent.

"Ayaan?" I walked toward him.

"I thought we decided we weren't going to talk to each other." Did he really take that conversation seriously?

"Are you hungry?" I couldn't help but ask, he seemed so tired.

"I'm fine." That wasn't the answer to my question.

"You look tired." I was about to say more when he grabbed my arm tightly and pulled me closer to him.

"Stop doing this!" he shouted at me.

"Stop doing what?" I fired back, fighting through the pain that I was feeling from his grip.

"You're driving me crazy..." His other hand softly stroked the side of my cheek.

"Ayaan." His touch was doing things to me. I was becoming weak around him. His strong, curious eyes were demanding me to tell him that I had locked up my heart so I could protect myself from heartbreak.

He suddenly let go, picked up his stuff, and went upstairs.

I was starving. Even though he told us not to wait for him for dinner, I wanted to eat with him, so I hadn't eaten what Huma had made. I wasn't about to wait for him now, though, so I went to the kitchen and reheated Huma's meal.

"You didn't have dinner?" Ayaan's voice unexpectedly came from behind, and I jumped.

I shook my head, put my food on a plate, and went to the table. After watching me for a while, Ayaan joined me at the dining table.

"I told you not to wait," he sighed. He reached for the food and started eating, and from the look on his face, I could tell he was enjoying it. At least I did something right.

We both ate in silence.

"Is everything okay?" I asked him when I noticed him reading something worrisome on his phone.

"Nothing that concerns you," he replied sharply, and again, I was reminded of my place in his life. "There is a tax problem at work and the issue might end up in court...my staff can't handle anything properly when I'm not in the office."

One thing I always knew and admired about Ayaan was his work ethic. He was a self-made man, and one of the most respected businesspeople in Karachi. He started his company from scratch and knew the ins and outs of his field. His mother helped him with his business from time to time, while also managing her law firm, so when she found out that Ayaan was returning to work, she went back to law full-time. That change was probably causing Ayaan some stress, too.

"Don't worry, I'm sure you'll fix everything." I also knew he was a determined man: Whatever he put his mind to, he always achieved.

"How do you know that?" He turned around to face me, waiting for my answer.

"Because I know you...and I know how much work you've put in your company. You won't let anything happen to it." I tried to encourage him, and, for the first time in an exceptionally long time, I saw him smile at me.

"Ayaan, can I say something?" Since he was in a good mood, I thought maybe it was a good time to discuss some things.

He nodded, waiting for me to continue.

"Please don't change...especially not for of me. I know you don't want me as your wife, but let me be your friend. I'm just as alone as you are, and if you think by acting coldly toward me and saying bad things to me will make me hate you, then you couldn't more wrong. I can't stand to see you in pain." I reached across the table and held his hand. I was going back on my promise to myself to not get emotionally involved, but seeing him alone and miserable hurt me more.

I wasn't going to let Ayaan give up on himself this easily; I wasn't going to let him destroy his life. Ayaan didn't deserve this punishment he decided he deserved, and

Mariam wouldn't have wanted to see him like this, either, if she were alive.

He studied my face for a while; there was complete silence around us. We had no excuses, no expectations, and no other people to pull us apart at this moment.

"We can't be friends, Noor." He pulled his hand away from me and walked out of the kitchen.

Chapter 10

Ayaan

Let me be your friend...I'm just as alone as you are...I can't stand to see you in pain...

Noor's voice kept echoing in my ears when I walked away from her. I knew she wanted to help me or she wouldn't have agreed to marry me. But I just couldn't remove Mariam from my mind or my heart. Everywhere I looked, I saw her. She promised she was going to be there for me and our child, she promised me to love me and grow old with me...

I closed my eyes and waited for sleep to take over, but it didn't. I kept tossing and turning and couldn't get myself to sleep, so I got up and went back downstairs. I walked out into the backyard and decided to call my mother.

My father and I have had issues since the day he decided to leave my mother and me. I forgave him, but couldn't get myself to love him the way I did before. My mother was a strong woman, so she didn't waste too much time grieving and accepted the fact that her husband was no longer hers. She showed kindness toward him and offered to let him to stay in my life so I didn't grow up without a father. But the reality was that the day my father walked away, my mother became a single parent and played the part of both mother and father, all while working and staying financially independent.

She was out of the country to attend some conference, but I dialed her number anyway, hoping she'd pick up.

"Assalam O Alikum" She answered the phone after a few rings.

"Assalam O Alikum, Mama...how are you?" I greeted her.

"I'm good...what are you doing up so late? Is everything okay?" she asked me. I looked at the time; it was nearly half-past three in the morning.

"I couldn't sleep...were you busy? I can call back later." I didn't want to disturb her or keep her away from work.

"No, no, I was just heading back to the hotel. You tell me, how are Noor and Hamza?" She was always fond of Noor. She used to tell Mariam and me that if she had had another son, she would have brought her home as her second daughter-in-law.

"They're fine. I'm sorry I didn't answer your calls earlier." She'd called me multiple times since the wedding, but I couldn't bring myself to talk to her. She was the one who'd asked me to make Noor my wife after Mariam's passing. I was too distracted by my own thoughts to oppose her decision—or any decision, for that matter—that I just did whatever seemed right by everyone.

"That's okay...I understand. I'm just glad you called." She understood.

"Why did you do it? Why did you make me marry Noor? She would have taken care of Hamza like a mother without marrying me. I want to know why you forced us into this nameless relationship?"

"Until when? Her parents would have married her off to someone else. Do you think after marrying some other man, she would have loved Hamza the same way she does now or been there for him every step of the way? And what about you? Would you have been able to take care of Hamza on your own? As soon as Mariam passed away, I knew you wouldn't be able to move forward in your life with anyone, but when I saw Noor holding your child in the hospital and the way she stayed up all those nights to look after him...I knew she was the right woman for you. And you only really need her as your companion."

I was speechless when she said that to me.

"Still...I just feel stuck. It's not fair for Noor. She had to sacrifice her life and dreams for us. I feel ashamed and guilty every time she looks at me...every time she tries comforting me...I feel like I should be the one supporting her, but I can't get myself to do that," I told her honestly.

We were silent for a long time after that.

"If you continue to feel like that, then I'm afraid things are not going to get better between the two of you. Only you two can fix this, Ayaan. She's young, she left her home for you and Hamza. Stop looking at her the way you used to when she was your sister-in-law; she's your wife now and you're her husband. Being comfortable around each other will take time, but in the meanwhile, try to understand her position, my dear," she continued.

"Are you listening?" she asked me, when I didn't reply.

"Yeah. I'm tired...I'll call you later," I told her.

"Sure. Just think about what I told you, and call me whenever you want."

I said goodbye and went inside the house. Before going to my room, I decided to check in on Hamza.

When I opened the door, I saw Noor standing near the bed. Her back was turned from me, and she was holding Hamza in her arms, humming something, probably trying to get him to sleep. At that moment, I saw a different side of Noor, a side I was too selfish to notice before. Mama was right; it wasn't easy to find a girl who would love your child like her own. But there she was, holding my child as if he were hers. She left her home for me and Hamza, but I never made her feel like she belonged here.

I was looking at her when she suddenly turned around. Her eyes popped open in shock when she caught me watching her. I was leaning against the doorframe, and it almost felt like I was a kid who got caught stealing something.

"I wanted to check if everything was okay."

I had to say something before I scared her.

"Yes, everything is okay. I was just trying to get him to sleep." She looked at Hamza; he was now quietly sleeping in her arms. I couldn't help but smile.

"I'll look after him, you can sleep." I offered, wondering how many nights she stayed up to make sure Hamza got his sleep.

"No, it's fine." She was too kind, too sweet. It didn't help me feel any better.

"Okay. Goodnight." I closed the door on the way out and went back to my room. This time, when I closed my eyes, I finally managed to drift into a comfortable sleep, feeling a new set of emotions that I had never felt before.

Chapter 11

Noor

I couldn't get back to sleep after performing my morning prayer. Hamza was on my bed playing with a toy, and Huma was watching him, so I closed the door behind me a bit and walked to the kitchen to make myself a hot cup of tea. There was nothing more serene than watching a beautiful sunrise on a cold morning with a hot cup of tea.

After pouring the tea, I went over to the bookshelf to grab the novel I was reading and sat right by the glass door in the sunroom, looking at the dark clouds that were slowly turning light.

"Mind if I join you?" Ayaan came out of nowhere, and I almost dropped my book. He was wearing the same clothes as last night when he got home from the office. He must have been too tired to change.

"Sorry." He half-smiled and sat on a chair right across from me.

I glanced over at him and saw him looking out at the dark sky, like the way I was a couple of seconds ago.

"What were you looking at?" He looked down from the sky to ask me.

"I don't know..." I whispered. It was so quiet that I could hear even the smallest of sound. His crisp voice, amplified.

“What are you reading?” He pointed at the novel. I showed him the cover. I still couldn’t figure out why he was asking me anything. We usually only talked to each other when it was required.

“A love story...what a surprise,” he muttered sarcastically.

“Why are you so bitter now? You were in love once,” I reminded him.

“And look where it got me,” he shot at me with a hurtful gaze.

I stayed quiet and grabbed my cup of tea to enjoy instead. It was a lot sweeter than his words.

“Have you ever been in love?” he asked, and I stared at him. We’d never talked about such matters before.

“What? It’s a simple question, is it not?” He shrugged his shoulders.

“I don’t know what love is. Frankly, I don’t even know if it even exists.” I gave him an apologetic smile.

“You should have ended up with someone else...not with someone like me.” He sighed.

“Well... I guess you’re stuck with me. Sorry.” I got to leave, but he grabbed my wrist to stop me.

“That’s not what I meant. Sorry, it came out wrong. Please, sit...” he requested, and I sat down again, waiting for him to say something.

“Noor, all the love I had in my heart...I gave it all away. But you...you deserve to be loved. You deserve to be taken care of. Your sister...she had so many hopes and dreams for you, and now your entire life is only us. Stop sacrificing your life for us. I'm already indebted to you." He looked down and I could see he was ashamed of himself. He felt like he wronged me.

"Say something...anything..." He kept his eyes on the ground.

"You don't always get a say in life. Sometimes things happen, and they take us by surprise. Yes, I wanted to do many things in my life. I wanted more time with my sister, most of all. But those are the things I wanted, and just because you want something, doesn't mean you'll get it. It doesn't work like that. In life, things happen: people grow apart, relationships fail, some dreams don't come true, people get left behind, and people...die...that's just the way it is. But what matters is that I'm still here, and so are you and Hamza. The three of us are still here, and we must learn to live without Mariam. I must accept that she's gone, and Hamza will eventually have to learn that his real mother was a great person, but unfortunately her time had come and she left us. We can't move on and grow if we continue to feel sorry for ourselves or each other, now can we?"

There, I said it. Everything that was boiling inside of me finally spilled out. Yes, it was a bitter truth, but someone had to tell him.

"What should I do?" When he lifted his head and I saw his face clearly, I saw tears falling down his face. I walked over to him and got down on my knees. I grabbed his face with my hands and wiped away his tears.

"We have to let go," I finally said. I couldn't help myself from crying after seeing him breaking like that in front of me.

“Noor...” He got up from the chair and pulled me up with him. His hands moved from my shoulders to my face, and he gently wiped away my tears.

“She’ll always be here.” I placed my hand on his heart. He placed his hand over mine and nodded.

“Come here.” He embraced me tightly and I put my arms around him. We stayed there, holding onto each other, and letting go of the person who would always remain special in our hearts.

At that moment, after a very long time, I saw a glimpse of the Ayaan I used to know. The one my sister fell for, the one I considered a friend, and the one who wasn’t a stranger to me at all.

Chapter 12

Noor

"Do you think we could go to my parents' house tonight? I was talking to Ammi this morning and she said some of our Baba's friends and close family members are gathering at their place for dinner. I understand if you don't want to go, but..." I mentioned to Ayaan over the phone, as he was in the office.

"Sure, be ready by seven," he cut me off, taking me by surprise. I didn't think he'd agree to it.

"Really?" I asked again to be sure.

"Yes, Noor. Anything else?" he spoke calmly.

"No. Thank you. I'll be ready by seven. Okay. Thank you. Bye!" I blabbered in excitement.

"Idiot," I murmured to myself after hanging up. I went to my room to pick an outfit. Finally, after almost two months, I'd be visiting my parents with Ayaan and Hamza together, formally.

"You look chipper." Huma entered the room with Hamza, who was giggling at something Huma had said to him. He looked at her as if he could understand what she was saying.

"We are going to my parents' place tonight," I told her.

"Ayaan agreed?" She sounded amazed as well. I nodded,

and her smile grew.

“That’s wonderful! I’ve noticed a positive change in Ayaan in the past couple of days. Even his behavior toward you is getting better. I’m very happy for you kids.” Her eyes sparkled.

Huma was such a caring, selfless woman. I adored her. Without her, this journey would have been a lot difficult.

“Yes, it’s getting better,” I hoped. Ayaan and I were in a much better place. We were trying to establish a relationship with boundaries, along with trust and goodwill toward each other.

“Why don’t you wear a saree? You are a newlywed.” She placed Hamza down on the bed, opened my closet, and pulled out a beautiful nude-colored saree with silver, pink, and aqua embroidery on it. I bought it a long time ago, but never got a chance to wear it.

“Here… wear this.” She draped the fabric around my shoulders.

“It’s a little too much. How about this?” I picked a light pink dress with shimmery white sequins on it.

“What time will he be coming to pick you up?” she asked me while putting the light pink dress back in the closet.

“Seven.” I looked at her, noticing how she swapped the light pink dress for the saree.

“You’re wearing this. That pink dress will see another day. You should start getting ready; I’ll get Hamza ready in the meantime.” She picked up Hamza’s clothes from the drawer and left the room.

I had already taken a shower this morning, so my hair was

slightly wavy. All I had to do was run a brush through it. I changed into the saree and put on red lipstick, a little concealer under the eyes, and some mascara. For jewelry, I wore white diamond-studded earrings.

By the time I was finished getting ready, it was already seven o'clock. I didn't know if Ayaan was going to need to change, but to be on the safe side, I went to his room and selected a light-blue striped blazer set for him. When I got back downstairs, I heard his car pulling into the driveway.

When he walked inside and saw me, he stopped. I glanced at Huma, who was smiling.

"Assalam O Alaikum," I immediately said and walked into my room. The way he looked at me, I felt strange, unveiled. I waited for a few minutes and slowly walked out, thankful he wasn't there anymore.

"Where's Hamza?" I asked Huma.

"He took Hamza upstairs with him," she chuckled. Huma knew I was intimated by him; she was getting a kick out of my misery.

Moments later, Ayaan walked downstairs with Hamza in his arms. He was wearing the clothes I picked for him. No matter what he wore, he always looked good. He was so unaware of his good looks that it made him stand out more.

"Ready?" He smiled at me. His demeanor was different. Good different.

"Yeah." I said goodbye to Huma and started heading outside when I heard him tell Huma that we'd be out late.

The ride was mostly quiet. I asked him about his day, and

he asked me about mine. When we got out of the car, he took Hamza.

"Take it easy. I'll look after him," he said to me. Was I dreaming?

"Noor," he spoke again when we approached the door. I turned my head to look at him.

"You look..." Before he could finish speaking, we were interrupted by my father who answered the door and welcomed us inside.

Ayaan didn't say anything after that. We were greeted warmly by everyone, and my parents were more than happy to see us together. We looked like a couple, complimenting each other nicely, according to my parents and everyone else at the function.

"Long time, no see, Noor." I heard a very familiar voice from behind, and I knew exactly who it was.

I turned around to see Maaz, the guy who rejected me three years ago when his family came to our house to ask my family for my hand in marriage. Maaz was a son of my father's friend. We used to be good friends when we were young, but when I found out that I'd never be able to conceive a child, Maaz rejected me, even though he once told me he loved me. I guess love wasn't enough for him to marry me. I forgave him, but he never stopped taunting me about it. His parents were nice people, so they apologized on his behalf, and because I never wanted my father to lose his friend, I never asked him to stop socializing with Maaz's family.

Why did he have to be here today, of all days?

"Maaz," I acknowledge him as I noticed he's walking toward me.

"Congrats on your marriage. How come you never invited me?" he teased.

"You were out of country," I didn't want to stoop to his level. I was better than that.

"Still, you should have sent me the invitation. Anyway, let's forget it. To be honest, I didn't think you'd ever get married," he sneered, and I looked at him with disgust. Baba was right, even if a person is educated or rich, it didn't guarantee good character. Maaz was both, but he was poor in character. It's crazy to think that I once considered him a friend, and even worse to think I imagined sharing a life with someone as shallow as him.

"Oh, c'mon now, you know I'm joking. I'm happy you got married. I heard you married your sister's widower...but hey, you got a free child." He looked at me pathetically.

"Why are you saying all of this, Maaz? What did I ever do to you?" My heart was hurt by his cruel words, but I smiled at him, anyway. I didn't want him to think that his words were affecting me.

Just then my mother joined us, and I quickly wiped away my eyes before she could notice the tears.

"Your mother told me you're getting married. Congratulations, Maaz!" She patted his shoulders.

I felt sorry for the girl already.

"Thanks, Aunty. The wedding's in three months. You'll be the first to get an invitation." He side-eyed me when he said that, and I looked down.

"Noor..." Out of nowhere, Ayaan was right beside me,

putting his hand around my waist. He was glaring at Maaz. Did he hear our conversation?

"Ayaan, this is Maaz. He's our friend, Mr. Iqbal Muneer's son. Maaz and Noor did most of their schooling together. And Maaz, this is Ayaan, he's Noor's husband," my mother introduced them to each other.

"Maaz...Maaz Muneer? You're the owner of Intercity Enterprise, right? Or I should say used to be? I heard your company went bankrupt last month. You must be in a lot of debt after paying off creditors and investors." At this point, I was certain that Ayaan heard our conversation from earlier and was now trying to belittle Maaz.

"Ayaan, I think..." I tried to interrupt, but I was cut off.

"It's all in the past. Let's leave business out of family events," Maaz managed to say.

"Oh, Mr. Khalid, what a pleasant surprise!"

Not again. This time Maaz's father was the one to join our conversation. I wanted to leave, but Ayaan held his grip tightly around me to keep me from going anywhere.

"Mr. Muneer. How are you?" He shook his hand.

"I'm okay. You must have heard about Intercity Enterprise? That issue is just testing our patience," he replied and Maaz stared at his father, trying to make him stop talking.

"You have many contacts, Mr. Khalid. Could you please help Maaz...oh, excuse me," he said, walking away to answer a phone call, leaving Maaz and his red face behind. My mother was still with us, looking between the three of us.

"Tell me, Noor, should we help Maaz, here? The poor guy is struggling badly. I'm afraid by the time he finishes paying off his loans, he's not going to have much to offer to his bride." Ayaan finally moved his eyes from Maaz to me.

I stared at him in disbelief. He knew that I knew what he was doing.

"Come on, Noor, his future lies in your answer." He smiled, looking satisfied. He wasn't going to let us go until I gave him an answer. When I gazed at Maaz, I saw humiliation and remorse in his eyes for the first time ever.

"Help him," I responded, pushing Ayaan's hands away and leaving to get some fresh air.

A while later, Ayaan came outside and sat beside me near the water fountain.

"Are you okay?" He shifted his position so he could see me. I kept looking ahead.

"You shouldn't have done that," I told him.

"And let him insult you like that?" He grabbed my arm to make me look at him.

"I was handling the situation," I informed him, snatching my arm from his grip.

"Yes, you were. Your comeback to his insults was quite impressive." He was being cynical.

"You don't know anything about this." I got up to leave, but he stopped me.

"I know everything. Your father told me," Ayaan replied, and I turned to look at him. My parents seriously couldn't keep anything to themselves. I felt ashamed of myself.

“Hey…look at me.” He came closer and cupped my face in his hands.

“You have no reason to feel bad about yourself, not even one. You’re perfect, you hear me?” He tried to get me to look at him by stepping closer to me.

“It’s not true,” I whispered. I wasn’t perfect. I wasn’t capable of having a child.

“You already have a child. Hamza is your child. He’s your son. You’re a great mother and he is very, very lucky to have you in his life…do you understand?” His eyes were soft.

“Yeah,” I nodded. His words comforted me, knowing that I had Hamza.

“Now repeat after me. Say ‘I’m perfect.’ Say it back to me,” he demanded playfully.

“Ayaan…stop it!” I held his hands to try to break free.

“Say it,” he repeated. He kept his eyes glued to me, not agreeing to leave until I followed his request.

“I’m perfect,” I listened to him, although I didn’t believe it. It did make me feel a little better, though. I followed it with a deep breath.

His hands dropped from my face, and he held my hand before I could even take a step away.

“Let’s go inside.” He caressed the back of my hand with his thumb. His touch felt so natural that it felt like it belonged to me.

“Ayaan…” I was about to thank him again for supporting

me when my mother called my name.

Before I could walk to her, Ayaan stopped me again.

“I didn’t get a chance to tell you earlier, but you look very beautiful,” he whispered, bringing his face closer to mine before walking away with a wry smile, leaving me completely flushed.

Chapter 13

Noor

"What did I tell you?" I heard my father's voice from behind. I was in his library looking at the books I used to read when I lived here. There was a layer of dust on some of the books that made me realize that time has passed.

He sat on his favorite brown leather chair, and I took a seat right across from him on the sofa. Everyone had left after the party and the house got quiet again.

At the party, Ayaan treated me how he'd once treated Mariam. Everyone looked at us as if we were a perfect couple. He looked at me warmly, spoke highly of me to my friends and other relatives. It made me even think more highly of him. I felt like he wasn't pretending, but that it was him—the real him—doing all those things for me.

"It got better, didn't it?" My father smiled, there was a sense of satisfaction and relief in his eyes. I thought about the time I told my parents that I wouldn't be able to stay with Ayaan. What if my father hadn't told me to go back? What would have happened?

"It's getting better." I looked down at my hands and saw my wedding ring. At first it felt like a burden, but now it was starting to feel like a part of me, an important part.

"You did that...I hope you realize that. We're so happy to

see you together like this. Your mother told me about what happened earlier with Maaz. Ayaan took a stand for you," he stated with pride and fondness for Ayaan in his voice.

"It still feels surreal, Baba. I'm not used to it," I told him truthfully. Every day with Ayaan was different. It felt as if we were both trying to find the missing pieces of a broken jigsaw puzzle and making an effort to put it back together one piece at a time.

"It has been thirty years since your mother and I got married, and we're still not used to it," he joked, and we both laughed.

"The times have changed. It was different when you guys got married. The constitution of marriage has evolved over the years. True love, love at first sight, fighting for love, being a hopeless romantic...these things don't exist anymore," I told him.

"Every marriage is different, my dear, and let me tell you one thing: Believe it or not, companionship and marriage may have evolved, but love is still love. Times may change, people may change, feelings may change, but love...it doesn't change. It can't change. It stays with you for as long as you want it to."

My father, yet again, left me completely speechless. No wonder my mother fell head over heels for him when they met in college.

A moment later the door opened, and Ayaan walked inside.

"Speak of the devil and the devil appears." My dad smiled.

"I hope she wasn't complaining about me." Ayaan sat

next to me and looked at me.

“No...I was just...we were...” I needed to practice getting used to talking to him without stammering.

“She was praising you, my son. She said you take good care of her,” my father stepped in, and Ayaan just nodded and looked at me again before continuing to talk to my father about other things.

Occasionally, I glanced over at Ayaan and saw how charismatic he was. The way he spoke to people, it made them feel important. It was a rare quality, one of many others he possessed.

“It’s quite late. I think we should get going.” Ayaan checked the time. It was quarter-past two.

“Why don’t you kids stay here tonight? In fact, stay with us for the whole weekend. We’ll get a chance to spend some time with Hamza, too,” Baba suggested.

“No, Baba, we’ll come over some other time,” I managed to say. We wouldn’t be able to sleep in separate rooms if we were to stay.

“I think it’s a good idea,” Ayaan admitted, his words throwing me off guard.

“Great...that’s what I wanted to hear!” Baba looked overjoyed. Ayaan didn’t think this one through.

“No, we can’t stay. I mean, you don’t have any clothes to wear or anything, and all of Hamza’s stuff is in the house. We’re not prepared,” I said, hoping he’d get the hint.

“That’s all right. I’ll tell Huma to gather our stuff, and the driver can bring everything here.” Ayaan shrugged as if what he was saying was no big deal.

It was a big deal.

My father left the library to get my old room ready for us to stay in, leaving Ayaan and me behind.

“Why did you say yes?” I turned around to question Ayaan, who had just hung up with Huma after telling her to pack our things.

“Why not? You like our house better than your parents' house now?” He put his phone away and placed his hand behind my head on the backside of the sofa as he leaned toward me.

“Ayaan, we'll have to stay in the same room here. You know that, right?” I finally stated what was bothering me.

“So?” He looked serious, as if he had no idea what the problem was.

“So...you're okay with us staying in the same room?” I copied his facial expression.

“Why would it not be okay? You're my wife. I ‘m your husband. That's what married couples do, Noor, they sleep in the same room.” He was staring at me as if I was speaking gibberish.

“I just thought...you weren't...we stay in separate rooms in our house.” Was I missing something?

“We can change that once we get back. You can sleep in my room.” He half-smiled.

“Are you only doing that because you feel sorry for me? Is that it?” Because he found out I couldn't have a child and felt bad?

“What? No. Why would I feel sorry for you? I don't feel

bad for you; stop looking down on yourself, Noor. You told me to learn and move forward...don't you remember the speech you gave that day? It put some sense in my head and I want to try...I want to try again, and I want you to try with me. Stop victimizing yourself. Now, answer me...do you have any problem staying in the same room as me?" He moved closer to me.

I shook my head and he nodded.

"Good." He got up from the sofa, and I followed him to out. As we both reached for the door, he stopped and glanced over at me again. "Don't ever think that I help you because I feel sorry for you...you don't need to be rescued. I do it because your reputation is important to me, and I won't let anyone point a finger at you...I won't stand for it."

He walked past me, and I couldn't move forward. Maybe it was easy for Ayaan to say all of that to me, but he had no idea what he just said. He made me feel worthy, protected, and cared for. He didn't love me, but he appreciated me, and that was more than what I ever imagined I was entitled to.

Chapter 14

Noor

I used the washroom downstairs, and Ayaan went to the one in our room to change. Baba wanted Hamza to sleep with him and Ammi, so I went to check up on them before I made some tea and took it to my room. Ayaan was looking through my college yearbook and smiling.

"Oh, god, I look terrible in those pictures." I put the tea on the side table and walked over to him to take the book from him.

"No, they're nice," he responded right away, pulling back, not letting me have it.

"I made some tea, if you want it," I offered. He closed the book and looked at me.

"Are you a mind reader?" he commented and picked up the cup.

"What?" I didn't understand.

"You're rather good at figuring out what I want." He passed another cup to me, and I took it.

"Well you're not that easy to figure out," I blabbed without thinking. I slowly glanced his way to see if he heard that...and he certainly had.

"I'm not an easy person to live with, either." That's all he said.

"But you're a nice man, Ayaan," I told him truthfully.

"Don't I know it," he proclaimed cockily, and it made me laugh.

"I didn't get a chance to thank you." He put his cup down and turned his attention to me. He walked over and stood in front of me.

"For what?" I wondered.

"For taking care of Hamza like that...for taking care of me. I didn't know how I was going to raise Hamza after Mariam passed away, but thankfully you stepped in and took charge of everything. You made it a lot easier." He took my hand in his and just held it. This touch was different; it meant something else. Or was it only my imagination?

"Ayaan..." I said his name softly, and he looked down at our hands. He let go and stepped away, as if he heard my thoughts.

"It's getting late," he pointed out before laying down on my bed. Good lord, he was on my bed. I stood there and waited. There wasn't even a sofa in my room.

"Are you going to stand there all night?" He popped his head up and stared at me. He kept his eyes on me while I walked to the bed and sat on the edge, as far away from him possible.

"Don't worry, I don't snore," he joked. "But I can go if you want...if you're uncomfortable," he said to me as his eyes bore into mine. I laid down next to him and turned around to face him.

"No, you don't have to leave...I feel comfortable around you." It was true, he made me feel safe.

"Good." He brought his hand up and slowly pushed my hair back from my face. He didn't say a word, but his eyes —damn those eyes, they were so expressive. What was happening between us? It wasn't sympathy or compassion or sorrow that we felt for each other...this was something else. A gut-wrenching, falling-from-the-sky-without-a-safety kind of a feeling. It was making me scared, excited, and emotional all at the same time. I'd never felt this before.

His fingers traced down from my cheeks to my chin, and his hands dropped. His eyes moved from my eyes to my lips as we both stayed silent in the moment.

"Goodnight, Noor." He looked at me in the eyes before turning his back and shutting off the light.

It was going to be everything but a good night's sleep when Ayaan was sleeping right next to me. Good gracious. I closed my eyes and tried my best to not think about what happened just now.

As I predicted, I stayed awake the entire night, and I was sure Ayaan stayed awake, too, because he didn't shift at all. The entire night his back was turned to me. I got up before dawn and headed out of the room to pray.

After I finished praying, I wanted to stay out of the room so Ayaan could sleep in peace at least for few hours, but my things were in my room, and I had to change my clothes, so I returned quickly to grab my stuff. As I entered, I saw Ayaan coming out of the washroom, but he was shirtless...oh, god. No, please...

"I..." Both of us spoke at the same time and stopped, waiting for the other person to say something.

Ayaan picked up a towel from the bed and put it around his neck.

"You need something?" he asked.

"This is my room, but yeah, I need clothes for Hamza...you know, to change."

Great, simply great, Noor.

He bit his lip to keep him from smiling. He found the situation rather funny. Ayaan grabbed the bag Huma packed for us and handed it to me.

"You're up early," I said to him.

"I couldn't sleep."

"I know, I noticed...I mean, I couldn't sleep, either. It was too hot...in the room. Maybe the air conditioner's not working."

Note to self: Learn how to speak to Ayaan without sounding stupid or intimidated.

"Hmm..." Again, he bit his lip to hide his amusing smirk.

"I'm going to go," I excused myself and left the room.

After getting both myself and Hamza ready and enjoying a beautiful sunny morning outside for a while, I went to the kitchen and found my mother cooking.

"Assalam O Alikum, Ammi." I hugged her from behind and she smiled.

"Hungry?" she asked and I nodded. I sat on the table and waited. As she finished setting up the table, Ayaan and Baba came in. Ayaan took a seat next to me, but he didn't acknowledge me at all. Thankfully, Baba and Ammi didn't notice his strange behavior. At least, I hope they didn't.

During the meal, Ayaan mostly stayed quiet. He only answered when he was spoken to. Was he acting like that because of last night?

"Hey, is something wrong?" I couldn't help but ask after my parents had finished eating and excused themselves.

"No." He tried to finish his food quickly. He clearly wasn't in the mood to talk.

"Well if it's about yesterday..." I started.

"Nothing happened yesterday, okay?" He finally looked at me.

"You were right, you're not an easy person..." I shook my head and got up to leave just as I hit my toe against the corner of the dining table.

Great, as if the day wasn't going amazing already...

"Hey..." Ayaan got up from his chair immediately and grabbed my shoulder to keep my steady.

"Oh, now you're talking. Well, thank you very much, but I'm fine." I pushed away his hands, and he just stood there watching me struggle.

"Argh!" I cried in pain. I gave up and stood there, avoiding his eyes.

"You're such a child," he sighed and placed his arms around my waist. I held onto his shoulder and he helped me sit down on the chair just as my toe started bleeding.

"Where are the bandages? You need to watch where you're doing," he commented, but I choose not to reply. I pointed toward a drawer and he picked up the band-aid.

"I'll do it." I snatched it from his hands, but he snatched it back.

"Such a child." He sounded annoyed.

"Stop calling me a child," I fired back.

"Then stop acting like one." He kneeled to put on the bandage and massaged my foot. I'm not going to lie, it felt really nice, but I was angry, so I didn't say anything. He looked up and waited for me to say something, but I stayed quiet and stared back at him blankly.

"What is it, Ayaan? What's bothering you now?" I couldn't help but ask as he got up.

"You won't understand...get some rest, Noor," he replied and walked away. I couldn't understand why he was playing mind games with me.

Chapter 15

Ayaan

Saying last night was difficult to get through would be an understatement. The idea of having Noor within an arm's distance from me drove me crazy. Occasionally I heard her tossing and turning, sometimes I heard the rhythm of her breath changing. She was awake, I knew it. I wanted to turn around and look at her, not to say anything, but just look at her.

I was always mesmerized by the way she carried herself. No matter what she did or said, she had poise and charm and endless beauty. She wasn't aware of these qualities in herself, but that made her stand out even more.

As the night went on, time slowly passed and morning finally arrived.

As soon as I got out of the shower, I saw Noor sneaking into the room. When she saw me, the way her eyes went wide for a moment before she dropped her gaze...I found her facial expression rather entertaining. Her cheeks went completely red, and when I got closer to her, she held her breath. The way the sunlight hit her face made her look ethereal. I couldn't even pay attention to what she was saying, it was like my mind shut off and my eyes decided to look at nothing but her. How could someone be so beautiful and not be aware of it?

“What is it, Ayaan? What’s bothering you now?” Noor asked me once I finished putting the bandage on her toe. How could I tell her what was wrong with me if I couldn’t figure things out myself?

I left the kitchen after giving her a vague response; a confusing answer, for sure, but that’s all I could think of at that time. I went back to my—our—room and opened my laptop to respond to some work emails, trying to distract myself, but I failed miserably.

Minutes later, the door opened again, and Noor walked in and stood in front of me. I continued working on the computer, hoping she’d leave, but she stayed, snatched my computer from me, shut it down, and put it on the table.

“Ayaan, I want to talk to you.” The way she said my name, it felt nice, as if it belonged to her.

I got up from the bed and stood in front of her. As expected, she took a step back. It was funny to see her being so demanding but also getting intimidated by me.

“I’m listening...” I stared at her, waiting for her to speak since she had my complete attention.

“Why are you behaving like this with me?” she asked me with a hint of frustration in her voice.

“Like what?” I asked her back. I knew what she was referring to, I just wanted her to ask me clearly.

“Sometimes you act like you care about me, and sometimes you don’t even look at me...is everything okay between us?” I never expected her to be so straightforward.

“That bothers you?” I took another step forward and grabbed her elbow to keep her from moving away from me. She didn't say anything back, just stared back at me with hundreds of questions and worries in her eyes.

"Why do you care if I look at you?" I asked. I wanted to know what she thought about me—not as her unchosen husband, but as a man.

"I *don't* care, I just don't get your mood swings," she answered quietly after I moved back a little to give her some space. I saw her eyes were completely shut, and I could feel her pulse running quickly under my grip.

"You're not in love with me, are you, Noor?"

Something made me ask her. I couldn't keep myself away from her...it was becoming rather impossible. I couldn't say I loved her, but yes, I was starting to like her. I didn't know how it happened, but anything she did...it affected me. There was an unknown connection between us, an indescribable one, but I needed to know what she thought about me first.

"What are you talking about?" Her eyes opened, and she looked at me with horror. She wasn't giving away much. Usually her eyes held thousands of words, but today I couldn't figure out what she was thinking, not even in the slightest.

"It's a simple question...do you like me, Noor?" I asked again. I couldn't move until she answered my question.

"I asked you a question first, Ayaan." She dropped her gaze and stared at the floor instead, attempting to avoid answering the question.

"It doesn't matter..." I didn't care who asked what. I wanted her to answer me immediately.

"I need to go to Hamza..." She tried to leave me, but I

pulled her closer to me.

“Baba and Ammi are with him. I won’t let you go until you answer me,” I commanded, taking charge. I had already started the dialogue and I wanted to see where it went.

“Why do you care if I like you or not...is it going to make any difference?”

Why wasn’t she looking at me?

“It will make a world of a difference. I care, that’s why I want to know. If you feel anything toward me, tell me now.” I realized I was almost shouting at her, so I lowered my voice and tried to speak easily.

“I can’t just give you an answer...I don’t know what to say.” She bit her lips out of nervousness. She was anxious. That’s exactly why I wanted to avoid her. She was confused and didn’t know what she felt for me. She wasn’t ready. God, I shouldn’t have done that. I didn’t want to force her into anything. I let go of her immediately and turned around so she couldn’t look at me.

“Ayaan…” Her small voice called out my name. What was I going to say now?

“Noor, please leave.” I tried to keep it together.

“Ayaan, don’t shut me out.” Her voice was breaking, and it shattered me.

“I’m heading out.” I quickly grabbed my wallet and phone and headed out the door before all hell could break loose. I didn’t want to ruin whatever good we had.

I didn’t mean to be playing mind games. The truth was, Noor had no idea what she wanted. I could tell she liked me. I knew it from the moment she melted in my arms when she thought I overdosed on diabetic medication and confirmed it when she said she couldn't see me in pain, and even last night when I touched her and her eyes sparked up with anticipation and longing. I could be wrong one time, even two...but every time we were close, there was a strange pull between us, and I knew she sensed it, too. Why couldn't she accept it?

Chapter 16

Noor

You're not in love with me, are you, Noor?

Ayaan's simple question caused enormous turmoil in me. The second he asked it, I knew I was doomed. The truth was, I wasn't sure. The way he asked me, though, pressuring me to give him an answer right then, didn't make me feel good, so I told him I didn't know, which was partially true. I respected Ayaan, I was fond of him, but was I in love with him? I didn't know.

"Hello?"

I heard a very recognizable voice and looked up and saw my friends Somiya standing outside my room.

"Oh, my God!" I shouted in excitement as I ran over and hugged her tightly.

"I can't believe you're here...when did you get back?" I asked. She went to Shanghai for a study-aboard program this past year and wasn't here when I got married. Everything happened so quickly that I didn't even get a chance to tell her the whole story.

"I can't believe you got married..." she said with a smile on her face.

"How did you find out?" I let go of her. We both sat on my bed, and I turned off the television.

"Aunty told me. Well, actually, Aunty told Mama, and Mama told me. I got back three days ago. You still look the same...except your hair." She noticed my hair had gotten much longer since the last time we met. She seemed happy and more confident; she was radiating such good energy that seeing her just lifted my mood.

"How was Shanghai?" I asked her.

"Good. My parents were freaking out about letting me go all alone, but the transition team at the college there was extremely helpful. I had so much fun! Enough about me though...what happened with you? You married Ayaan? I didn't believe it at first when I found out."

It's crazy how Somiya and I used to tease Mariam with Ayaan's name to make her blush before she got married, and now we were here talking about my marriage to him. I looked at Somiya when she mentioned his name, but there was no hint of judgement in her voice. She was genuinely curious, not just looking for gossip.

"Mmhmm...Hamza needed me, and I wanted to raise him and be there for him, and this was the only way." I gave her the simple answer.

"How is Ayaan? Does he treat you well?" she asked me.

"He's fine...he misses Mariam a lot. Even though he doesn't say it, I notice it. I catch him staring at her picture in the living room when he's about to leave for the office and sometimes he picks up her books just to hold them as if he can feel her essence. But then he tells me he's trying to move on, and I don't know if I can believe that."

Maybe that was the reason I couldn't answer his question earlier. Even if I felt something toward him, did he feel the same way too? What if we were both on a different page of the story?

“Ayaan really loved Mariam, but he also cares for you. Even before all this, he used to look out for you and always knew when you were upset before anyone else.” She smiled at me. She was right. “He’s a good man,” she added.

“He is.” I returned her smile and we moved on to talking about other things.

Five hours had passed and there was no sign of Ayaan. I tried calling him, but he wasn’t answering. Was he okay?

“Why don’t you leave him a voicemail?” Somiya asked while we were having lunch together.

“No, it’s okay...he’ll be back.” I put my phone away and continued talking to her.

A few minutes later, I looked out the window to see Ayaan getting out of the car. As he walked in, his eyes met mine for a moment, but he dropped his gaze and moved to the other room.

He didn’t say anything, so I stayed where I was instead of going after him. If he was going act like that, then so was I.

“I sense some tension. What happened?”

Somiya should have been a spy.

“Nothing, he has crazy mood swings sometimes,” I pointed out sarcastically, and she chuckled.

After finishing our lunch, we walked over to the living room and saw Ayaan playing with Hamza while Baba and Ammi were talking to each other.

"Assalam O Alikum, Ayaan," Somiya greeted him chirpily. She walked over and picked up Hamza.

"Walikum Asalam. How are you, Somiya?" he asked nicely.

"I'm good. I can't believe you remember my name." She was surprised. They had only met a few times, and that was years ago.

"I have a good memory," he replied politely.

The entire time we were sitting together, he didn't look at me at all. Not even once. I knew I shouldn't care, but I did. I hated that even more.

"Excuse me." I got up, and this time he glanced at me as I walked past him.

My heart was feeling heavy; I didn't know if it was stress or an emotional imbalance or straight-up frustration. I went to the washroom for wudu, came out, and picked up a praying mat to start praying. It was the best meditation for me. It helped me clear my mind and heart. I asked for strength, clarity, and peace. I wouldn't say all my worries were gone afterward, but I felt a strange feeling of satisfaction and calm. I closed my eyes and took a deep breath. When I opened them and got up, I saw Ayaan entering the room, and he stopped as soon as he saw me.

He walked past me without saying anything, and I wanted nothing more than to shout at him and ask him where he was and why he didn't call me, but I didn't. Him ignoring me felt as if hundreds of thorns were slowly stabbing me. I hated him for making me like that. And the worst part was that the further apart we were, the more the pain increased.

"You've been awfully quiet today," my father pointed out at the dinner table.

Somiya left to be with her family, but she promised me that she'd visit me soon. Meeting an old friend after so long felt so good. I felt as if I could finally share my feelings with someone without fear.

"I'm not feeling well...just under the weather," I told my father. Telling him everything was okay would have been a lie, so I told him half-truth hoping to get away with it without having to answer more of his questions. That's all I had been saying all day, only half-truths.

"Should I make you some tea?" Ammi asked me. I shook my head and continued with my meal in silence.

"Why don't you guys take a vacation?" my father asked out of the blue, and both Ayaan and I looked up from our plates and stared at him. I remained quiet and waited for Ayaan to say something.

"It's up to Noor. We can take one if she wants to," he answered.

"The reason I'm bringing this up is because there's a charity event in Bulgaria that your Ammi and I are invited to attend by the funders, but I have some conflicting meetings with the council. I would love it if you guys could go there on our behalf."

"When is it?" Ayaan asked him.

"Next week."

"I can move things around in my schedule..." He nodded and peered over at me.

"What about Hamza? I don't know if it's a good idea to..." I started.

"Huma can look after him, or he can stay here with Ammi and Baba," Ayaan jumped in.

Ayaan's got to be bipolar, right? He purposely ignored me for an entire day and now he's agreed to go to Bulgaria with me.

"So, should I confirm your attendance?" Baba asked.

"Of course. Right, Noor?" There was a challenge in Ayaan's voice. When I looked at him, my mouth got dry. What was going on with him?

I nodded with doubt, but he had a small grin on his face for the rest of the meal.

I had completely lost my appetite.

Chapter 17

Noor

"We'll drop by before you guys leave for the trip," Ammi said to me as my parents walked us out to the car.

"Okay." I took Hamza from my mother's arms and Ayaan opened the door for me.

Despite it being quite late at night, the streets were awfully quiet. Usually in the city, even close to midnight, the shops and most street vendors had their businesses up and running, but today was different for some reason. Most of the stores were closed and there was a weird silence on the streets.

"Did you hear anything on the news before we left?" Ayaan asked suddenly. He noticed it, too. I hoped there weren't any riots going on nearby.

"No. Hold on, let me check." I turned to grab my purse from behind my seat to scan the news on my phone.

"Three people were shot near the four-square plaza. I think we should go back to my parents'...it's not safe...I don't see a lot of cars." I looked up from the phone to Ayaan, who was looking straight out to the road.

"Ayaan," I called his name louder this time and he turned to me.

"It's okay, we'll be home soon." He sped up the car.

Sadly, riots like these were common here in Karachi, as many political parties often had clashes like this, and cultural terror fueled fear in society. Because of it, the public had to suffer. Like many cosmopolitan cities, it was still developing, learning, making mistakes and redeeming itself time and time again by growing businesses and welcoming dreamers from all over the country.

We were about ten minutes away from our house when, out of nowhere, a couple of bikes started following us.

"They're following us, Ayaan," I told him, and he didn't respond. Instead, he stopped the car.

"What are you doing?" I grabbed his arm as he was about to get out of the car.

"They're not going to do anything. Besides they'll either attack us here or follow us to our house." He took my hand and removed it from his arm.

"Ayaan, please, don't do this. I'll call the police. Just stay here. Don't leave me," I grabbed him again. "Don't get out of the car. Stay here, you hear me?" This time, he shrugged my hand off him and got out of the car.

I turned around and saw him walking into the empty alley where the bikes had stopped. It was dark since all the streetlights were off, so I couldn't see outside properly. After twenty minutes had passed, I noticed Ayaan's phone was still in the car. My hands were ice cold and my throat went completely dry in fear. How could Ayaan leave me like this? How could he be so selfish? If anything were to happen to him, I wouldn't be able to handle it.

I had to check on Ayaan. I didn't care if anything happened to me, but I wanted Ayaan and Hamza to be safe.

I covered Hamza with a light blanket, and moved to the driver's seat. I drove the car right in front of the alley. There was no one there except the bikes. I stepped out of the car and locked the door. I ran further into the alley, but it was completely empty. I looked everywhere, but there was no sign of anybody. I often heard stories of people getting kidnapped and being lost forever, so I collapsed on the ground and hugged myself tightly.

This couldn't be it. I couldn't lose him, too. He can't leave me.

"Noor," I heard Ayaan's voice say and it brought life back to me again. When I turned around and spotted him standing a few steps away from me, I couldn't move. I had once heard someone say life had flashed before their eyes, and today I experienced it.

"Noor," he said my name again, and I stared at him. He was alive! He was okay!

"Hey..." he rushed over to me and pulled me up to stand. My legs were still shaky, so thankfully he didn't let go of me.

"I told you to stay in the car." He took my face in his hands.

"Let's just go." I removed his hands from my face and ran back to the car, having a hard time catching my breath. Didn't he value his life at all? How could Ayaan decide everything for himself and put his life in danger without even considering Hamza and me?

The rest of the ride home, we didn't say anything to each other. I couldn't stand to look at him. I kept wiping away my stupid tears—they weren't stopping no matter how hard I tried. As he parked the car in the driveway, I immediately opened the door and jogged inside to my room to find Huma sitting on my bed reading the holy book.

"Noor?" She looked worried as she saw me. She put away the holy book and walked over to me.

"What happened, dear?" She touched my cheeks, and I hugged her tightly and started crying. "Did Ayaan say something to you? What happened? Tell me…" She patted my head, but I still held onto her.

"Ayaan what did you say to Noor?" she asked him, and I knew he must be behind me. I didn't want to look at him.

"Noor…" he said my name softly, but I ignored it. He took Hamza to his room, and when I knew he was gone, I let go of Huma and sat on the bed. Huma grabbed a glass of water and passed it to me.

"Thank you." I drank the whole glass.

"What happened, Noor?" She examined my face again.

"He left and he didn't even think about me...not even once," I whispered.

"Noor?" She didn't quite understand what I was talking about.

"Because of the riot, everything was shut down around the four-square plaza, and as soon we got there, some people started following us. And do you know what Ayaan did? He stopped the car and went after them, leaving me and Hamza behind. He didn't even say anything or even think about us for a second," I told her and she smiled.

"Why are you smiling?"

"He wanted to keep you and Hamza safe." She smiled again. How could she be so calm all the time?

"If something were to happen to him. I would've never felt so alone in my life," I stammered.

"Don't think too much about it. Ayaan has always been like this. He's selfless and he's protective of the people he cares about. Now stop crying and go change...there's dirt on your clothes."

"He only cares about himself!"

I opened the drawer and noticed that my clothes weren't there, then I checked the closet and those clothes were gone, too.

"Where's my stuff?" I asked Huma.

"Ayaan moved your stuff upstairs to his room today and told me to stay in here from now on."

And I thought I was done with surprises for one night.

"He came here today?" I asked, and she nodded. So that's where he was for the entire morning. Again, he made this decision without even talking to me. He didn't even ask me if it was okay to move my stuff to his room.

Why are you testing my patience? I looked up at the ceiling and walked out of my old room to what was apparently my new room.

Chapter 18

Noor

There was so much I wanted to tell Ayaan; so much to ask him. But I couldn't—not because I didn't know what to say, but because I was afraid that if I started, I wouldn't be able to stop.

I was sitting on the edge of the bed while Hamza was sleeping calmly next to me in his crib. I stared at his beautiful face. He had Mariam's eyes. Knowing that a part of my sister existed in Hamza brought so much joy to my heart, and being able to call him my son was one of the biggest blessings of my life.

I was deeply consumed in my thoughts when the bedroom door opened and Ayaan entered the room. He had changed into a black t-shirt and khaki-colored trousers. He looked at me for a brief moment but didn't say anything. Instead, he picked up his laptop and sat at his desk, turning his back to me.

Was he angry with me? I'm the one who should be angry.

I didn't feel like sleeping, so I walked out onto the balcony and stared out at the quiet roads and the sea waves that you can see from our house.

I heard the glass door sliding behind me, and I turned to see Ayaan stepping out. He closed the door behind him.

"Are you still upset with me?" he asked.

I shook my head and turned my attention back toward the road. Say something, Noor. You wanted him to talk to you, so why were you quiet now? Get it together.

Before he could leave, I called out his name and he stopped.

"I was scared," I managed to say. My heart was beating so fast. I clasped my hands together and took a heavy breath to calm my nerves.

He approached me and touched my elbow to turn me.

"What did you say?" He leaned in closer.

"I was scared." I looked down because I didn't have the confidence to look at him. I never felt so shy in front of him.

"Why?" Ayaan brought his hand to face and pulled my chin up. I shifted my gaze from the ground and saw an unreadable expression on his face.

"You should have stayed with us, Ayaan. If something were to happen to you... When I got out of the car to look for you...you weren't there and I thought something had happened." I didn't even know what I was saying. I was mostly mumbling through my tears. Such a mess.

"Noor," Ayaan said my name softly and pushed my hair behind my ear.

"Ayaan, don't ever risk your life for me. I'm not worth saving. You should have thought about Hamza before getting out of that car. He needs his father. Those people could have killed you." Without realizing, I grabbed his t-shirt by the shoulder. When I noticed what I was doing, I went to pull my hands away, but Ayaan took them in his and pulled me closer.

"How many times do I have to you that Hamza needs you as much as he needs me, if not more? You don't get to tell me whose life is worth risking for whose. Now tell me honestly, why were you actually crying earlier?"

"I already told you...I was scared." I tried to pull my hands away, but he held them even tighter each time I tried.

"That doesn't answer my question. I know what I saw. I just want to know from you if what I saw was the truth or whether I'm misreading things." He was being so direct. I didn't know he paid such close attention to me.

"I thought I lost you," I answered truthfully.

"I hate to break it you, but you're stuck with me, Noor. I 'm not going to let go of you that easily." He half-smiled and wiped the tears away from my face.

"Please promise me you won't do anything like that again. Please…" I pleaded. At that moment, while standing in that alley searching for Ayaan, I had never felt so vulnerable.

"I'm sorry I can't make that promise, but I do promise that I won't let anything happen to you or Hamza." He let go of my hands and took a step away from me. His eyes, however, still stayed on me. We came to the point of the conversation where we had no idea what to say to each other. There was still so much that was left unsaid.

"Did they hurt you?" I asked him.

"Come and see for yourself."

Ayaan took me by surprise when he suggested such an offer. Was I dreaming? He couldn't have just said that to me.

"What?" I blinked. Perhaps this whole thing was in my imagination.

But it wasn't. It was very much real.

"I said see for yourself." He walked toward me again and kept walking forward until my back hit the balcony railing. He placed both of his hands on either side of the railing, blocking me.

"Ayaan." That's all I managed to utter.

"Yes?" He continued to stare at me, making me feel more nervous.

"You should get used to this," he commented.

Get used to what?

"To me looking at you," he answered, as though he heard my question. He bit his lip. Oh, God, it was cold outside, but I was as warm as an oven.

"Ayaan, please," I begged and looked down, not knowing what else to say. I didn't expect our talk to go this way. He chuckled and grabbed my hand to take me inside.

As we were walking down the hallway, I noticed that the pictures of Mariam that were framed in his bedroom before were now gone. Ayaan had probably taken those down when he moved my stuff here today. I was too occupied thinking about him to notice anything else.

"If you took down those pictures because of me, Ayaan, I don't want you to think that I..." Before I could finish, he cut in.

"I know that. Don't feel bad about it. Those were just pictures; she's still with us in our hearts. Hamza's growing up and you're here. Both of you are the truths in my life. I want Hamza to grow up knowing you as his mother, and I can't have you sleeping on my bed with Mariam's pictures on the wall," he answered.

Hamza was smiling in his sleep, perhaps having a good dream. It made us both smile as well. We looked at him and then at each other.

"I don't want to take her place." I climbed on the left side of the bed and laid down, leaving Ayaan standing in the middle of the room. He turned the lights off and came to lay on the bed with me

"You don't have to take anyone's place, Noor. You have already made your place." Ayaan responded and closed his eyes.

My eyes stayed on him for as long as I could keep them open and when I closed them, I still imagined Ayaan—his handsome face and that tender look in his eyes—before I fell asleep.

Chapter 19

Noor

"Thank you so much, Baba and Ammi, for taking Hamza to stay with you."

Ayaan and I were leaving for Bulgaria the next morning and my parents were taking Hamza to look after him in our absence. For the past couple of days, Ayaan worked overtime to get his work done so he didn't have too much to catch up on when we returned from the trip.

"Oh c'mon, we need excuses to spend time with Hamza. It's not a problem at all." My mother smiled and glanced over at Hamza who was being fed by Huma in the living room. Huma gets tired after doing all the housework, so I didn't want to leave Hamza with her while we went on the trip, otherwise she would have been completely drained.

"I emailed you the hotel and venue details," Baba mentioned.

"Actually, I canceled the hotel booking. Noor and I will be staying there longer, probably for a week, so I rented a house instead. It'll be more comfortable." Ayaan looked at me, and I stared back at him. He hadn't told me that. I thought we'd only be staying there for two days.

"A week?" my father asked.

"Yes, I have some new business prospects in Bulgaria that

I'd like to meet while I'm there. I was planning on going there later this year, but now I have time, so I thought it'd be best if I get that out of the way. Noor can accompany me while I'm there and learn about the business," he replied, and my mother smiled. She was clearly pleased with this change of plan.

"Noor told me there was an incident after you left our house last week. What happened? You should be careful, Ayaan." I told my mother everything. I didn't give her all the details, but I did ask her to talk to Ayaan about it—maybe he'd listen to her.

"It was nothing, Ammi. Noor probably exaggerated; she gets too worried. When the bikers started following us, I knew there was a police station close by, and I know the inspector there. I texted him and he was already out in the alley by the time I got there. The guys had guns, but they didn't have any bullets or anything. They just used them as a prop to scare families...you know how these people are. When the guys approached me in the alley, I ran toward the station. On the way, my friend caught them, and we went to the police station to do paperwork."

"Why didn't you tell me all this?" I glared at him, and my parents were looking at me. I asked him the same question yesterday, but now that my mother asked, he gave the whole story.

"What's done is done. Let's just forget about it. Thank God everyone is okay," my father jumped in and handled the situation. I shifted my attention back to the plate and didn't look at Ayaan throughout the entire dinner, although I could feel his eyes on me for the most part.

"Thank you, Huma, for such a lovely meal. Everything was just wonderful." My father was right, Huma was a great cook. She had a great passion for it, and you could see that in the dishes she made.

"I have packed some food for both of you, I'll go get it." Huma went to the kitchen and returned with two bags filled with food.

"Huma, this is too much." My mother took the bags from her, looking at how much she had packed for two people.

"This is nothing. The kids will be gone tomorrow, how am I going to finish all this food?" Huma took Hamza in her arms and kissed his cheeks, and he happily wrapped his entire hand around her finger.

"I will miss you, my dear." She stroked his cheeks and kissed him again before handing him over to my father.

"Please come over anytime, Huma, and call us if you need anything," Ammi told her, and she nodded.

"Okay, well, we better get going. It's getting late."

Ayaan took Hamza in his arms, kissed his cheeks and handed him over to me.

"Dear, it's just for a couple of days, don't cry." Ammi gently patted my back. I nodded and she took Hamza from me.

"Take care of Noor," my mother told Ayaan.

"Don't worry." He opened the door for my mother and my parents drove away.

Huma went back inside, and Ayaan turned to follow her, but when he saw me standing still, he stopped.

“Let’s go inside,” He lightly touched my shoulder, and I looked at him. I had never left Hamza alone for that long.

“Can’t I stay here?” I asked Ayaan.

“Noor?” He turned me around so he could see me.

“I’m always with him. How am I going to…”

Before I could finish, he placed his finger on my lips.

“If you stay here, how am I going to survive there?” His response left me speechless. No, I must have misheard it. Was this his way of saying that he’ll miss me if I ever leave?

“But you’re used to it. You spend most of your time out of the house anyway,” I replied. Ayaan probably said that without thinking too much of it.

“Just because I’m used to it doesn’t mean I like it. When I come home, I know you’ll be there.” He held my hand and looked into my eyes. My heart started beating so fast. Whenever he was near, I felt as if my heart would explode.

“I just know that I’ll miss Hamza. A lot.” I didn’t know what else to say.

“Won’t you miss me when I’m gone?”

“I have to start packing.” I pulled my hands away from him, but before I could walk away, he grabbed my wrist again and pulled me back to him.

“Tell me if you’d miss me if I went away.”

I glanced away from him and nodded, unable to meet his intense eyes.

“I can’t live without you, Noor. I don’t know if it’s a habit or dependence or something else, I just know that I can't manage without you."

I was so worried to face him. Every word he said was breaking me more and more.

"Baba and Ammi are with Hamza, and Huma is also here if anything happens. I want us to go together," he quickly changed the topic, and I relaxed a little.

"I'm going with you," I assured him, pulled my hands away, and turned to leave before he could stop me again or say something that would leave me tongue-tied.

"Good. Besides, what's the point of going on your honeymoon alone?" I heard him say from behind and I froze.

Did he just say honeymoon?

"Coming?" he whispered in my ear so suddenly that it made me jump.

"What did you say?"

He winked at me, walked past me and went inside, leaving me with my crazy heartbeat, making me nervous as hell. His nearness always made me anxious, but I was able to avoid him here. How was I going to keep my distance from him there? I took a deep breath and followed him inside. My worries were reaching a whole new level.

Chapter 20

Noor

As soon as we arrived at the rental house in Bulgaria, I was completely mesmerized by how beautiful it was. It was simple, spacious, and had an old-fashioned interior. It was a three-bedroom house, with a beautiful wooden-floored kitchen, a stunning patio, and a small garden with wildflowers.

"What do you think?" Ayaan joined me with our luggage as I was checking out the closets in our bedroom.

"It's beautiful." I smiled widely at him.

"The event is tomorrow evening; I'm going to go pick up the car and get some food...can you...?" He picked up his phone.

"Put your clothes away? Yes, I will," I finished his sentence. I was starting to understand him as each day passed by. Some aspects, I would say, not all.

I spent some time talking to my parents while he was away, asking them about Hamza and telling them about where we were staying. After the call, I spent the rest of the time unpacking our stuff and walking around in the garden, enjoying the weather and the change of scenery.

About three hours later, Ayaan returned with a mini car and some essential groceries.

"I'll prepare the food. Why don't you go and change?" I took the bag from him and walked to the kitchen.

"Let's go out to eat." He followed me.

"Aren't you tired? We don't have to go out. I'll cook something," I told him.

"Well, you must be tired, too. Skip the cooking and go get ready...we're going out." He didn't wait for my answer and left the kitchen.

I used the spare bathroom to change into black trousers and a plain white shirt. I put on some light makeup and combed out my hair, too. By the time Ayaan got out of the washroom, I was already ready. He was dressed in a nice navy blue and grey striped shirt and a pair of black jeans.

"It must be a stereotype..." Ayaan walked around the bed and sprinted some cologne on himself. He smelled amazing.

"What?" I had no idea what he was talking about.

"That all women take hours and hours to get ready." He half-smiled.

"Not all..." I sat there waited while he dried his hair and made few calls.

"Let's go." He took my hand as he finished his call. Even at the airport, he held my hand the entire time. It didn't feel bad, but it felt strange. The way he secured my hand in his felt as if he was scared to let go or afraid that I'd pull my hand away. I tried to ease my hand in his, but I couldn't.

The drive to the restaurant wasn't too long. In less than thirty minutes, both of us were happily sitting in a small cozy Italian restaurant with our margherita pizzas.

“Penny for your thoughts.” His voice startled me. I was overanalyzing everything. My thoughts were clouded.

I shook my head and looked out the window. This place was magical: It was a type of place I read about in books. How did I end up here?

“We have to start telling each other things, Noor,” he insisted, and I looked at him.

“I do tell you everything,” I responded. I mean, mostly.

“Do you have an outfit for tomorrow?” He changed the subject. He didn’t believe my answer, but I didn’t want to talk about it. I had nothing to say, and I didn’t want to ruin whatever was between us.

“Yes, I think so.” It was my first time going to a charity event, so I wasn’t too sure what to pack, but I did bring few options that I thought would be suitable.

“It’s a black-tie event, so if you don’t have a gown, I can take you shopping tomorrow morning,” Ayaan offered.

“I have some clothes that will be suitable. I don’t think shopping is necessary.”

“Let me put it this way…I’m taking you shopping tomorrow morning,” he ordered. Neither of us said anything after that. We quietly finished our food and got into the car to drive back to our place.

“Have you come to terms with this marriage, Noor?” he cut the silence, and his out-of-the-blue question left me startled.

“What do you mean?” I pushed the hair behind my ear—something I did when I felt awkward. His boldness was making me feel embarrassed.

“I mean, have you accepted me as your husband or is this still a compromise for you?” He parked the car and locked the door, trapping me inside the car with him.

“Ayaan!” I almost shouted. Why was he being so childish?

“Tell me.”

“What do you want me to say? Tell me what you want to hear, and I’ll say it back to you. Why are you even asking me this? Weren’t you the one who said that although we are married, you would never consider me your wife,” I quoted his words from the night we got married.

“A lot has changed since then, don’t you think?”

“Has it?” I asked.

Whatever he wanted to say, I was ready to listen. He stared at me for a while and closed his eyes.

“Not like this,” he murmured, unlocking the door and exiting the car. I stayed in the car for a while to work out exactly what happened before following him inside.

The rest of the night, he mostly occupied his time by doing virtual meetings for work from the living room while I stayed in the bedroom and tried to watch television, but my mind was somewhere else. What did Ayaan mean when he said not like this? Why couldn’t he just say what he wanted to tell me? The good, the bad, whatever it was. His hot and cold behavior was confusing me.

I heard his call end before he entered the bedroom. He noticed me looking at him, but he looked like his mind was elsewhere. He slowly walked toward the bed and sat down, his back to me. So now he couldn’t even look at me?

“I can stay in a different room if you want.” I don’t know why I said that, but quiet Ayaan worried me more than angry Ayaan.

“I didn’t say that,” he blurted out, still not looking at me properly.

“We always end up coming back to square one, huh?” I bit my lip, trying to hold myself together. I was breaking from the inside.

“You know why that is?” He finally turned and his eyes met mine. I didn’t answer his question. “It’s because when I take a step forward, you take a step back.”

He looked hurt when he said that. Was I wrong for feeling scared and nervous at this stage in our relationship?

“I’m sorry.” That’s all I managed to say.

“Noor.” He took a deep breath and came closer to me. “What are you so afraid of?” His hand gently pushed my hair behind my ear and stayed on my cheek.

“I don’t know what I feel. I can’t stand being around you, and I get scared when you leave me. I wait for you when you’re gone, but when you’re close to me, I feel like running away from you because being with you drives me crazy...”

He wanted me to tell him everything, so I did.

“I sound crazy…” I shook my head and pulled back from his touch.

“No, you don’t...you sound like me.” He smiled.

“What?”

“Well, I used to feel like that...now I don’t, because I figured it out.” His eyes were saying a lot more than his words. There was a spark in them, one that suggested he’d figured out the world’s greatest mystery.

“Figured what out?” I asked. My curiosity got the best of me.

“You’ll figure it out for yourself, though I think you might already know.” His smile was gone now. He looked serious.

Was this his way of saying that he had feelings for me? No, Noor, don’t go there. It’s not possible. Ayaan will always love Mariam; he can’t possibly fall in love with you. But what if it *was* possible? What if Ayaan was falling in love with me? He said whatever I was feeling, he used to feel the same way. Did that mean that I was also going to fall for him? Or had I already?

Before I could fully digest his response, I realized that our bedroom lights had switched off and Ayaan was deeply asleep right next to me. As if I was not in a dilemma already. How was I going to figure this out, whatever this was?

Chapter 21

Ayaan

She kept looking my way, but never uttered a single word over breakfast. Each time I looked up from my plate, I saw her looking at me, completely lost...her eyes glued on me, but still appearing indecisive. I coughed, and suddenly she blinked, coming back from whatever she was thinking about. Her cheeks flushed, she bit her lip and looked down, her beautiful long hair shielding her blushing face. Oh, Noor, how could you not know that I had fallen for you?

"Ready to go?" I spoke first. I knew she wasn't ever going to talk unless spoken to. She was a stubborn girl, but I don't think she knew just how stubborn she was.

"I already told you that I have some dresses. We don't have to go," she replied, still not meeting my eyes. She was pretending to focus on cleaning the table.

"I wasn't asking." I picked up my phone and walked outside to the car. I needed her get her talking.

A few minutes later, Noor walked outside, dressed beautifully in a plain white dress and a leather jacket.

I knew she caught me staring at her, because whenever she did, she shyly pulled her hair behind her ear.

I opened the car door for her, and she gracefully stepped inside...continuing to avoid my gaze. Why wasn't she looking my way? Did I really say something so wrong that she had nothing left to say to me? Should I speak to her about last night?

No, not yet.

I pulled the car out of the driveway and started driving. Occasionally, whenever I glanced over to check up on her, I found her either with her head leaning against the window with her eyes closed, her delicate fingers tangled in the fabric of her dress, or with her with her eyes wide open, admiring the beauty of this city.

"How many places have you traveled to?" she asked out of nowhere. This time, her eyes were closed again, and her head was leaning against the window.

"A lot of places. I've lost count. Why?" It didn't really matter why, I wanted to speak to her any chance I got. After marrying her, I realized how little I knew about her likes and dislikes. Of course, before our marriage, we had our fair share of conversations, but they were never serious or felt this important.

"Just wondering. What's the most beautiful place you've been to?"

"I don't look for beauty in a place, I look for a connection." I answered and stopped the car at the light.

"Is there a connection here?" Her voice sounded clear this time. She was looking at me now.

"Like no other." I held her eyes. We kept staring at each other, as if we were fighting, testing one another. I heard a car honk from behind and I saw that the lights had changed. I spotted a nice shopping alley just ahead and pulled over.

"I see some boutiques here. Shall we?" I turned off the engine and we headed out to explore the shopping area. The first two boutiques had nothing special. They had good clothes, sure, but nothing good enough for Noor.

The last boutique, however...

"This one?" She pulled out a plain black dress.

"No." I refused and walked to the couture side of the store to find a dress that caught her eyes earlier.

"Noor..." I called out her name and she walked over to me. By the look on her face, I could tell she was uninterested and clearly wasn't enjoying this shopping trip.

"Excuse me, miss, please pack this one in her size." I pointed at the mannequin wearing one hell of an exquisite dress. The store lady looked at Noor for measurements and went to pack it up.

"You can't just decide for me like that," she told me.

"Then who can decide for you?" I asked back, and she gritted her teeth. I cleared my throat to keep me from laughing, knowing she would get more upset.

"You know what I mean." She turned to leave, but I stopped her.

"You will look great in it. Don't you like it? I saw you checking out the display when we got here." I told her and she seemed impressed that I noticed.

"It's too expensive. You know I'll never get a chance to wear it again. It's a waste of money." She was so careful with her words these days.

"Then we'll just have to look for more parties to go to."

By the time we finished the conversation, the dress was already packed and ready for purchase at the counter.

After our little shopping trip, I drove further into the city near the downtown area. Noor was back to looking conflicted. I couldn't stand that look on her face. Whatever she was thinking, I needed to know.

"Are you okay?" I finally asked.

"Yeah, why?" She glanced up from her hands.

"No, it's just your behavior...you seem uninterested..." I stated.

"I'm sorry for behaving like that, Ayaan...I'm just not used to these types of things. I don't feel comfortable at big parties. I get anxious." By the look on her face, it was easy to tell that she was telling half the truth. I knew there was something else going on in her mind, too.

"I'll be there with you," I pointed out. She nodded and looked down again.

After walking around downtown, we went to a small coffee shop. It was mostly empty, but the smell of coffee was divine. We gave our order and I knew that the hard part was next…talking.

"You can't be Noor…" I didn't know what I was saying. I couldn't explain it correctly, but it got her attention.

"What?" She seemed confused by my statement.

"Well, the Noor I know doesn't stay quiet for this long. She speaks her mind, fights back...this Noor right here is nothing like her." I scooted my chair closer to her and she pushed her hair behind her ear.

"Do I make you nervous?" I asked her. She shifted in her seat and shook her head. "Of course, I don't," I teased her and she glared at me. Now we were talking.

"Don't challenge me," she replied. The nervous look on her face was now replaced with attitude. She never failed to surprise me. If only she could look at herself through my eyes.

"I just did, and I was right. I do make you uneasy?" I laughed and her face reddened.

"You don't. I'm just under the weather and you dragged me out here wasting my time. I'm not nervous; I'm just tired. Why would I be tense around you?" She spoke in a high-pitched voice and held her head up high.

"That's the most you've said all day. You sure you're not nervous? Or you are saying all that to hide it?" I mocked her some more.

"You..." Before she could say anything, the waitress returned with our order.

"Would you like anything else, sir?" the waitress asked.

"No, we're fine for now." I purposely smiled extra big at her, noticing Noor shifting her eyes between me and the waitress. "What are some popular spots around the area that we must see?" I tried to extend my conversation with the waitress, who kindly played along.

"Well, there's the Rila monastery, the national museum, the beaches...so many local restaurants, boutiques and hiking areas close by."

The waitress recommended some great places, but Noor's facial expression was the most entertaining of all.

"We'll surely check them out, won't we, hubby?" Noor spoke and smiled flatly at the waitress.

"Yeah, we will. Thanks, Amelia," I thanked her using the name on her tag, and she left. Noor gave her a strange look as she walked away; I couldn't help but laugh again.

"I know you did this on purpose," I commented, and she took a bite of her sandwich.

"What?" Noor pretended to look clueless. But her cheeks were glowing red as if she'd been caught cheating on a test.

"Hubby?" I repeated her words.

"So what? You're my husband; I can call you whatever I want." Again, she held her head high and stared at me with full confidence.

"Right...so you consider me your husband?" I asked her the same question from last night.

"Of course," she replied. "I mean...we're married. So, you *are* my husband," she corrected herself when she realized what she had admitted.

"That means I can also call you whatever I want?" I asked her innocently.

"I guess so." She stirred her tea over and over, probably thinking about everything that she had said to me, quietly reminding herself to think before she says anything in the future.

"How about I call you...a chicken?" I tried to say in a serious tone.

"What?" Her eyes went wide, and her mouth opened for a second to say something more, but she closed it.

"What? You called me hubby in front of that waitress because I'm your husband and per what you just said, you can call me anything you want. So the same rule applies to me. You're my wife, and I want to call you chicken" I took a sip of her coffee and she pulled her cup away from me. My wife was very much on edge at this point.

"I'm not a chicken." She smiled for a second, but frowned again.

"You are to me. You see, a chicken runs away, just like you. You get scared, and then you attack me for getting scared. Then when I tell you something, you always say no. See? You're a chicken." I pinched her nose and she slapped my hand away.

"Okay, fine, tell me to do something and I'll do it. But after that, you can't call me a chicken. Not ever." Her eyes were pure fire. She wanted to challenge me? I was all down for that.

"Nah, you'll get scared again. Like a chicken," I taunted her again so she wouldn't even consider backing down. If there was anything I knew about Noor, it was that if you challenged her, she would go all out to prove her point.

"Okay, fine then let's make a deal." She extended hand, and I looked at it, then back to her face. This absolutely gorgeous, crazy, stubborn girl was all business right now.

"You sure you won't back down?" I asked before extending my hand.

"I don't go back on my word," she spoke with full self-assurance.

"Okay, Noor, it's official. You must do whatever I tell you, and if you disagree, I'll start calling you a chicken." I held her hand and shook it.

"Fine, but if I win, which I'm sure I will, you'll never call me a chicken or any name like that ever again." She held my hand tighter.

"Of course, now for final confirmation. Let's seal it with a kiss..."

Before she could pull away, I kissed her hand.

Chapter 22

Noor

Ayaan's behavior since we got here was playing tricks with my mind. I didn't know what to think of it. I was happy to see him returning to his old self, but his affection toward me was making me anxious. I still had some doubts and insecurities, and I was scared to share those with him for some reason.

"I think we should start getting ready. The event starts in two hours, and it's quite a long drive there." Ayaan put away his laptop while we were lounging around in the living room watching some TV.

"Okay." I turned off the television and went upstairs to our bedroom to get dressed, and he followed me.

"Did you talk to Baba?" Ayaan picked up his nicely steamed black suit from the bed.

"Yes, they're fine. Hamza got his first tooth!" I told him, and he smiled widely.

"The little guy is growing up so fast. He'll be running in no time." Ayaan casually took off his shirt and I turned around, so my back was facing him.

"Chicken..." I heard him say under his breath, but still clear enough for me to hear it.

"Ayaan!" I threw a pillow at him, grabbed my dress, and

went to the washroom to change.

The dress he bought for me was indeed exquisite: a satin emerald green floor-length formal gown with long sleeves. It was elegant and hugged my curves perfectly. It was perfect. The zipper at the back was too low for me to secure by myself, so I left it open and moved to the makeup table. I blow-dried my hair, did a winged eyeliner, and completed the look with red lipstick and spritz my favorite perfume that smelled like freesia and black current. After spending a little over half an hour of standing in the front of the mirror and trying to make everything look flawless, I was finally ready.

I stepped outside and saw Ayaan sitting on the edge of the bed busy tying the laces of his shoes.

"Can you do me a favor?" I asked, and he turned in my direction. He scanned me up and down with his eyes.

"Can you zip up the dress? I can't reach it," I asked shyly, feeling his powerful gaze on me.

He walked behind me and moved my hair to the side. His fingers traced down my entire back. I felt completely exposed in front of him. My heart started beating so fast and my hands got sweaty.

"Do you like the dress now?" he whispered softly in my ear, and it sent shivers down my spine.

"Yes," I trembled and moved away from him as quickly as I could as soon as he pulled the zip up on the dress.

"I'll go get my purse." I needed to leave the room—the walls were closing in on me.

"It's right here." He pointed at the clutch that was on the bed. Damn it.

"We should leave now." I picked up the clutch and went closer to the door.

"What about the tie?"

"What about the tie?" I asked him back.

"I want you to tie it." He marched closer to me until my back hit the door. "Here." He took the clutch from me and handed me his tie.

"Is this your dare? After this you won't call me a chicken, will you?" I placed the tie around his neck.

"If you think this is a dare, then I'm afraid you have no idea what's coming." He bent down and got so close to me that we were practically hugging.

"Ayaan..." I hummed his name softly. My hands were still around his neck and I could feel his hands on both sides of the door, capturing me.

"You smell amazing." Ayaan moved his face to my neck; his trimmed beard tickled my skin. I pushed him back slightly.

"We're going to be late." I quickly tied his necktie, snatched my purse from him and left the room. I couldn't keep myself together in front of him.

We reached the event just in time. According to Ayaan, we were seated with one of the most important people in the business. Ayaan was a natural around business-minded people. He attracted talent and spoke in a way that left people in awe. As the event approached its end, he already had four new business contacts.

"How do you do it?" I asked him when he excused us from

a small circle of people to get some fresh air.

"Do what?" He picked up two glasses of sparkling water as we headed into the garden. It was beautiful, to say the least. The venue was almost castle-like, and this was probably the most stunning garden I'd ever seen.

"Don't be so humble about it. I'm talking about the way you are with people. How do you get them to listen to you like that?" As an introvert, I always struggled to make friends. Ayaan, however, was always the center of attention, no matter where he went.

"I pretend to be smart and most people buy it," He answered with humility, though I sensed a hint of embarrassment.

"That's not true," I came to his defense.

"No?" He stopped walking and sat on one of the empty benches by a small pond.

"I'm not going to praise you if you don't want me to." I sat next to him and he laughed.

"There's a draw tonight," he mentioned after a while.

"What for?" I inquired.

"Well, all the attendees tonight take part, and whoever wins gets 50,000 lev to go the charity of their choice."

"Wow! I hope we win then."

"We will," he confirmed with confidence, and I rolled my eyes. "We'll win."

"How can you be so sure? There are hundreds of people here," I stated the obvious.

"I trust my instincts, and I know we'll win tonight." He

looked at me.

"We'll see…" I didn't want to dampen his excitement.

"You don't believe me?" He feigned shock.

"All I'm saying is that you shouldn't have such high expectations. What if you lose?"

"You think I'm going to lose?" he pressed.

"Oh, God, Ayaan…you're unbelievable sometimes. It's a draw; it's all luck. All I am saying is that you shouldn't have high expectations…what if someone else wins? I wouldn't be so sure if I were you." I took off my shoes since the heels were starting to hurt my feet.

"Can't a guy and his instincts get some support here?" He looked down at my feet and then his gaze traveled up to my face.

"I won't support you because you're being silly." I stared back at him.

"Fine, mark your words, then. Because when I win, you'll have to do as I say." He got off from the bench and picked up my shoes.

"Keep on dreaming…"

I put my hand on his shoulder, took my shoes from him and put them back on. How could Ayaan be so confident about such a thing? There was a strange look of satisfaction on his face, almost as if he had already won.

"Let's say if you do end up winning tonight, what will happen?" I asked to play along.

"You can't go back on your words now, Noor." He was practically buzzing.

"Ayaan..." I shot him a look of dread.

"Noor..." He shot back the same look.

"Tell me."

"Okay, fine. If I lose, I won't call you a chicken anymore. But if I win, all you have to do is kiss me," he smirked.

Just then I happened to miss a step up the stairs, and he caught me.

"Careful now, you don't want to hurt yourself right before the challenge." He pulled me up to steady me and went inside the hall still with a hint of smirk on his face.

"Do you need some water, ma'am?" a waiter asked.

"No, I'm fine," I told her politely.

"Your face is all red, ma'am. Are you sure you don't want some water?" The waitress smiled sweetly at me and handed me another glass of sparkling water before leaving me alone with my embarrassment and panic.

I stayed outside for few minutes to calm down before chugging the glass of water and stepping inside to find my not-so-noble husband, whose foot I desperately wanted to stomp on.

Chapter 23

Noor

"Where were you?" Ayaan asked as I sat next to him at our table.

"I couldn't find the table," I lied.

"Sure..." He looked straight ahead and seemed serious as he continued socializing with other people at our table.

A while later, the host of the event, a young man named Mathew, came to the stage again and asked for our attention. It was time to announce the winner of the draw.

"Good evening, ladies and gentlemen. Before we announce the winner tonight and wrap up the event, we would like to thank all of you for your support and call out a few special people who made generous contributions in tonight's charity event."

The host started listing people who donated the most amount of money tonight. I wasn't paying enough attention until I heard Ayaan's name. I jerked my head to the side and looked at Ayaan, who was looking rather uninterestingly at his phone.

I kept glaring at him until he finally noticed.

"What?" he asked.

"I was with you this entire time. When did you donate all this money?" I demanded.

"It was done online."

"Due to the generous donations tonight, we decided to choose our draw winner from the three people who donated the most to our cause: Simon Baker, Okechuku Conwell, and Ayaan Khalid..."

I almost choked on my water.

"Looks like chances are one in three now, rather than hundreds," Ayaan said smugly.

"It's still possible you might lose." I tried to keep my voice strong and unbothered but failed. Instead it came out trembling.

"If you truly want something, nothing can keep you away from it, and I really want this." His eyes shifted from my eyes to my lips and back again. I broke our eye contact immediately. How dare he control my mind and heart like that?

His eyes were too intense for me at that moment. I couldn't think of a comeback, and he knew it.

"Okay, here it is. Let me just get the envelope... And the person who will be donating 50,000 lev to charity of their choice is...Ayaan Khalid from table 42!"

Everyone looked at our table. Before Ayaan got up to go on the stage, he winked at me, and a devilish smiled appeared on his face.

Assuredly, he walked on the stage and won the entire audience over with his witty jokes and a thoughtful statement on social responsibility and ethical business practices. As he walked back to the table, he was stopped by more people who wanted to talk to him. I was so proud of him. Not only he was a great businessman, but he was also an impactful leader who cared about people.

"How was it?" he asked me as the crowd started to thin.

"Do you really have to ask? You were brilliant, as usual!" I smiled widely at him.

"You seemed impressed." He scooted closer to me and placed his hand on my back to lead me outside.

"I'm extremely impressed. You did the right thing by donating tonight. Baba would be really happy to hear that," I complimented him as we got inside the car.

"And winning, you forgot that part," he pointed out, and I closed my eyes in embarrassment.

"How can I forget if you're here to constantly remind me about it." I rolled my eyes and he laughed.

On our way back to the house, we mostly kept the conversation fairly light.

"Can we stop and get some coffee?" I asked him. The truth was, I didn't want to go home. I was too nervous to even think about kissing Ayaan. I wanted to put off him bringing up the challenge again at any cost.

"You don't even drink coffee," he countered.

Right.

"I meant tea..."

"We're almost back to the house; I'll make some for us when we get there."

He sped up the car and turned on the radio. I had to think of something to keep him from bringing up that challenge again.

"No, I think I will just go straight to sleep. I'm really tired; I can't even keep my eyes open."

Maybe if he knew I was tired, he would stay away. How stupid was I to agree on such a childish bet?

"Well you can sleep now if you like. I can carry you to our bedroom."

"I'm not *that* sleepy." Oh, God, what was wrong with him? Did he know that I was trying to keep him away?

As soon as he parked the car in the driveway, I rushed inside.

"Noor…" I heard him calling out my name, but before he could come inside the room, I grabbed my pajamas and locked myself in the washroom.

"Noor!" he shouted my name this time.

"Ayaan, I'm in the washroom," I called back and finally relaxed when he didn't say anything further. But as soon as I reached to unzip my dress, I realized that I wasn't going to be able to reach it. Why did he have to buy me such a complicated dress?

"Ayaan…" I shamefully pulled my head out to ask for his help only to find him in nothing but his pants. He was half-naked, oh lord. I closed the door again and remained inside the washroom.

"What is it? Are you okay?" He knocked on the door.

"Yes, I'm fine…I just need help with the dress again." I kept the door locked.

"Well I would love to help you, but if you haven't noticed, the door's locked." I could tell from his voice that he was smiling. He was enjoying this.

"It can wait. Sorry I called you when you were changing. You can change your clothes, I'll wait." My heart was pumping really quickly. It wasn't that I minded seeing him shirtless, the problem was him knowing what his closeness was doing to me.

"Okay, I'm decent now, you can open the door," I heard him say after a while.

As soon as I opened the door, Ayaan marched inside the washroom and shut the door behind me. He lied; he was still very much indecent.

"You said you were dressed!" I tried looking anywhere but at him. He could have at least covered his upper body with a towel or something.

"And you said you were tired and couldn't keep your eyes open, and yet you spent the past fifteen minutes being locked away in here." His eyes bore into mine, and I took a step back. "Come here…"

Before I could move away from him any further, he hooked his arm around my waist and brought me closer to him. I placed my hands on his shoulders to maintain at least some distance, but every time I tried doing that, he kept pulling me closer.

"Now how about that kiss?"

His hands traveled up my back and he unbuttoned and unzipped the top half of my dress before securing his arms around my waist again.

"Ayaan...you..." He stopped me.

"Chicken." He pushed me back against the door and placed both his hands on either side of my shoulders.

"Don't call me that. I'm not a chicken."

"Then prove it." He inched closer to me, his eyes stopping on my lips.

"Fine." I grabbed both sides of his face and slowly placed my lips against his.

Chapter 24

Noor

In my dreams, I'm always running away from something or someone. Whenever I stop and look behind me, I see a shadow of someone, but before I can see the face, I always wake up. Last night, I finally saw the face of the person from whom I was running. It was Mariam. Why would I suddenly see her in my dreams after all this time? I couldn't sleep after that. I stayed in bed, staring at the blank ceiling—even the thought of leaving this room alone scared me. I waited until dawn and, as the light started peeking into the room, I glanced over and saw Ayaan sleeping peacefully.

Last night was such a blur. I knew I kissed him, and he kissed me back. I kept my eyes closed the whole time; I was afraid to look at him. I didn't know what I wanted to see in his eyes. I felt his hands slowly leave my back as he pulled away and left the washroom. By the time I mustered up the courage to enter the bedroom, he was already asleep—or at least pretending to sleep.

I guess neither of us really knew where we stood in this relationship, or what we wanted.

A few hours later I was walking around in the backyard and I heard Ayaan calling my name.

"I'm out here!" I yelled, and he came outside looking fresh and happy.

"Here..." he greeted me with a cup of coffee.

"You said you wanted coffee last night, didn't you?" he pointed out, and I couldn't help but blush.

"I did." I took the cup from his hand, thanking him.

"Was that your first kiss?" he asked as he sipped his cup of coffee.

Was he serious?

"Ayaan..." I looked at him with disbelief.

"Sorry to break it you, but your kiss wasn't as good as I expected." He tried to keep a straight face as he said it.

"Well I didn't see you complaining about it last night," I fired back at him.

"You could use some practice." He moved closer to me.

"I thought it was great," I defended without thinking.

He grinned.

"Oh, God." I laughed and was about to walk away when he pulled me back.

"Okay, fine, I won't mess with you again. At least stay here with me until I finish this."

"Okay, but drink fast." I tapped my fingers on the table.

"Why?"

"I have to clean the bedroom and make lunch," I answered him shyly, and he smiled again. "Why are you smiling like that?" I wasn't annoyed, I just felt like I wasn't getting the joke.

"You always look for ways to run away from me. You're not much of a romantic, are you?" He put down his cup and grabbed my hand.

"Noor?" He shifted forward and looked into my eyes.

Ayaan was a straightforward man. He said what he felt, and he expected the same. Sadly, I wasn't like that. Not only I was an introvert, but I always had trouble expressing my feelings.

"It's not like that. I just...it's new for me, Ayaan. I've never felt this way, and I don't know when I'll be able to give you whatever you expect from me." I looked at our hands and the way his fingers were entangled with mine.

"Don't be afraid of this. That's why I wanted us to come here alone. Whatever doubts you have about me, or us...I'm willing to work on it. Now and always. You're not alone anymore. Don't put so much pressure on yourself to make things right. If anything, it's me who needs to set things straight. And if we fail, we'll try again and keep trying until we get it right. I just want you to be happy, whether it's with me or..."

"I've never been happier," I stopped him and placed my other hand on his cheek. In return he also touched my cheek with his hand. He smiled and gently touched his head to mine.

"See? That was simple, wasn't it?" He pondered lovingly and I nodded, keeping my eyes closed, feeling him close to me.

"I still think you need some practice kissing," he recommended, and I couldn't help but laugh at his mischievous ways.

"We have our entire lives to practice now, don't we?" I opened my eyes and saw him inches away from me. His beautiful brown eyes boring into mine.

"Will you pull away if I kiss you right now?" His passionate gaze raised my body temperature.

Instead of giving him a reply, I closed my eyes, inviting intimacy. My heart was beating faster than usual, but that feeling was starting to feel normal, because my heart always pounded faster when he was close to me.

Seconds later, I felt his soft lips on my forehead instead of on my lips. They lingered on my head a few seconds longer than I expected before he pulled away and our eyes connected once again.

"What was that for?" I couldn't help but ask.

"You must really like me, although you'll never admit it," he commented. I didn't understand what he meant.

"What makes you say that?" I looked back at him. Of course I truly really liked him, but I still wanted to know what he was thinking.

"Well, first, when I went to kiss you just now, you held your breath. Second, last night, when I kissed you back, you kept your eyes closed even after I pulled away as if you were waiting for me to kiss you again. And third and foremost, last night when I dared you to kiss me, you could have kissed me anywhere—on my cheeks or my forehead, even my hand—but you kissed my lips. How does that sound to you?"

He bit his lip. I loved it when he did that. I almost forgot what to say to him for a moment.

"Sounds like you're very observant for a guy."

My face reddened.

"That's because you're too inattentive for a girl, which is one of many things I like about you." He pulled away slightly and brought my hand close to his lips.

"You like the things about me that I've always felt cautious about."

How was it possible to have a man like him, such a high-quality man, to be in love with me?

"That's because you don't see yourself through my eyes, but I'm sure one day that time will come and you'll understand that the things you feel self-conscious about are the things that make you you." He pecked the back of my hand and got up from his chair, and I peeked up to see where he was going.

"Although I would love to sit here all day and look at your beautiful face, we have to clean up the mess in our room. I think we should go and get some cleaning done." He pulled me up.

Once inside, just as I was about to take a step up the stairs, he swiftly picked me up in his arms.

"Ayaan..." I squeaked in surprise.

"The first time I carried you in arms was because your foot hit the table. It was purely for health purposes. Now let me redeem myself and do this properly. I've seen it in the movies, and it's rather romantic don't you think?" He tried to keep his voice steady, but I noticed he was out of breath just after taking the few steps. I couldn't help but laugh at him.

"Put me down; you'll drop me." I was serious. There were too many stairs and I was starting to question his strength.

“Stop looking at me with your hungry eyes. Let me focus,” he teased me.

“I’m not looking at you with hungry eyes,” I stuttered and he chuckled. Finally, he reached the final stair and put me down. I saw him panting. I tried to keep a straight face, but couldn’t.

“How do they do it in the movies?” Seeing him saying that in a serious tone did something to me and I started laughing hysterically.

“Stop laughing,” he ordered, but I didn’t listen.

“You should have seen your face when you said that,” I managed to say in between my laughs.

“Noor, stop laughing,” he warned me again, but it made no difference. In a blink of an eye, he grabbed my hand and pulled me closer to him and I gasped.

“It’s not so funny now, is it?” he whispered near my ear, making the hair on the back of my neck stand up. His hands moved from my elbows to my waist and he started tickling me. I yelped and ran away from him as he followed me, our laughter echoing through the house.

Chapter 25

Noor

"Ayaan, can I ask you something?" I smiled at him as he placed our order on the table and sat across from me in a lovely café.

It was still quite early in the morning. The days spent with him here were going by way too fast and a part of me wanted to stay here forever. Maybe I was scared that this wouldn't last long once we returned to our home. Between my caring for Hamza and his working around the clock, we would quickly go back to being our old selves. We wouldn't have time for each other at all.

I felt selfish thinking like that, but I couldn't help it. We slept in the same bed, talked for hours and hours until one of us went to sleep first, we cooked for each other, we waited for each other, our relationship had grown but we still weren't...close.

"What is it?" He took off his sunglasses and gave me his full attention.

"When do we go back?" I asked.

"Where? Back home?" He arched his eyebrow. I nodded.

"Couple of days—three or four...why?"

"Nothing..." I took a bite of my strawberry pancakes and looked out the window. I saw some kids playing soccer in front of a local department store.

“If it were nothing then you wouldn’t have asked…there’s always a reason behind your questions,” he stated.

I smiled, feeling glad that he was starting to understand me more, as I was understanding him better as each day passed.

“I just wish we could stay here forever,” I told him honestly.

“We can,” he responded. I didn’t know whether he was being serious or not.

“Then I’m going to miss my parents.”

“We can bring them here, too.”

“Are you serious?” I asked. He nodded.

“And what about your business?” I took a sip of his coffee. Funnily enough, coffee was growing on me just as much as Ayaan was.

“A lot of people take care of their businesses from different countries. That’s not a problem.” He dragged my plate toward him and ate my leftover pancakes.

“You’re willing to move everything here just because I said I want to stay here?” I looked at him with amazement.

He nodded innocently, and I wanted to hug him. How selfless was he?

“Don’t do this, Ayaan.” I took his hand in mine.

“Do what?” he asked with innocence in his eyes.

“I just told you that I want to stay here, and you agreed just like that, without thinking twice about it? Don’t you think it's a little...unrealistic?" I was glad to see Ayaan putting so much faith in me, but I had never seen any man who's willing to leave everything behind for a person like that.

"I want you to have everything that you desire. If moving here makes you happy, then I won't think twice about it. Look, I'm...I don't know if this is the right time for you to hear it, and I don't expect you to say it back, but I'm a simple man and I want to be honest with you. When we got married, both of us had many doubts in our minds, but now...I don't. I don't know when or how I started liking you and then suddenly, I had fallen in love in love with you and I thought I would feel bad or feel guilty about being in love with you, but I don't. When you walked into my life, I was broken, and you, in some ways, reminded me of Mariam, and in many other ways, you didn't, and I felt conflicted about it. But being with you here, I've realized I want nothing more than to be with you and grow old with you, and it doesn't matter if we're rich or poor, here or back home, sick or healthy...I only wish to be with you because you make me happy, Noor."

He took my hand in both of his and his lips curved in a gorgeous, heart-melting smile. I couldn't stop looking at him. I was trying so hard to keep myself from crying in the café.

"I love you," I whispered to him and tears started streaming down my face.

"Let's go." He smiled widely as he got out of his seat.

"Where?"

He seized my hand as I followed him out of the café into the unknown.

“I’ve just remembered something,” he responded as we made our way through the buzzing alleys in the area.

“What?” I asked. What could possibly be that important right after that important moment in our relationship?

“Wait...it was right here...somewhere.”

We reached a terribly confusing alley that had many different types of shops. We kept walking until he stopped and took me inside a small jewelry shop. As we entered, we were greeted by a very lovely old couple—owners of the shop, I presumed.

“Oh, you came back!” The old man walked around the cash register and his wife smiled at me as if she knew me.

“Yes. Is it ready?” Ayaan asked the old man.

“Ahh, yes, I kept it for you. Let me go get it.” The man grinned at me before going inside his workshop in the back.

“Dino was about to call you to remind you to pick up your order,” the lady told Ayaan. I still wasn’t sure what was going on.

“Here it is.” Dino returned with two wooden boxes and handed them over to Ayaan.

“Great! Thanks, Dino and Rosa.” Ayaan acknowledged the couple and took me aside in the store.

“What’s going on?” I glanced at the boxes he was holding.

“Well, we have to make this official now, don’t you think?” He smirked and opened the boxes. Inside were two beautiful rings. One was silver, and the other was rose gold with a stunning morganite center.

"Ayaan, when did you...how?" I was in complete shock. When did he plan all this?

"Don't keep me waiting! Give me your hand, please, Mrs. Khalid." He took my left hand in his and slid that gorgeous rose gold ring on my finger. It was such a magical moment for me, to love someone with so much passion and have that person mirror the same.

While holding Ayaan's hand, I realized how much value he brought to my life. He was my husband, my confidant, my friend, my home, my companion, and my lover all in one, and there would never be a person I'd be able to love as much as I loved him. The ring he gave me then was an endless promise that meant forever, and there was nothing I wanted more than to share my days and nights with him.

Chapter 26

Noor

"You can stop looking at it now." Ayaan smiled at me and took my hand in his as we exited the jewelry shop. Both of us now had our new rings connecting us, showing the world that we belonged together.

"I can't help it. It's beautiful. I knew you were romantic, but I wasn't expecting this at all." I squeezed his hand tightly, feeling indescribable joy, as well as the warmth of his skin against mine.

"That was the whole point. I like seeing your face when you're surprised. You blush a little, you get nervous and then you break into your world-famous smile," he said to me. I could sense him enjoying this experience, too.

"My smile is not world-famous," I stated.

"It is for me. I'm your biggest fan," he whispered as we approached a small park.

"And I'm yours."

"Of course you are. I mean, look at me," he teased, and I slapped his shoulder lightly.

"We have to go shopping tomorrow." We sat on the small bench by the sidewalk. My legs were hurting from all this walking. Wearing heels was not a good idea.

"For Hamza?" he asked, and I nodded. I did pick up some

things, but there was still so much I wanted to get for him. Our flight back was two days from now and I wanted to get him some new clothes, since he was growing out of his old ones.

"You're the one who named him Hamza," Ayaan uttered out of the blue. When Hamza was born, I was asked to pick a name for him. It's usually mothers who name their child, but instead Mariam trusted me with it, almost as if she knew I was going to become his mother one day.

"Yes...I get worried sometimes, though." I looked at him and he looked at me with curiosity in his eyes. "One day when Hamza grows up and understands that I am not his real mother...how will he feel? Will he distance himself from me?"

"How long have you been thinking about this?"

"A while."

"He's going to find out one day, and he'll love you even more," Ayaan replied with confidence, like he'd already thought about it.

"How can you be so sure?"

"I just know. Noor, having negative thoughts and worrying about things like that will only make our lives more difficult. No matter what people say, no matter what I say, you do what feels right to you, okay?" His fingers brushed over my cheek.

"You're officially my therapist. First it was Baba and now you," I told him and we both laughed.

"Are your feet hurting?"

"No..." I put my heels back on.

“You’re a terrible liar. Let’s go and find some better shoes for you. You don’t even need heels; you’re taller than the Eiffel Tower,” he stated with a straight face and playful eyes.

“Ayaan…” I snatched my hand away from him and got up to leave.

“Hey!” he caught my wrist and pulled me back.

“What?” I yelped. I wore heels so we complement each other, but he made fun of me instead.

“I love you.” He kissed my cheek and my entire face went got warm in embarrassment. Public display of affection was not my thing at all. I stayed quiet and rubbed my cheek where he his lips had touched it.

“Looks like I’ve found a way to shut you up.” He grinned.

“I won’t let you kiss me next time.” I held my head high.

“Yes, because you’ll kiss me before I kiss you,” he fired back. I hated his comebacks sometimes.

“That’s not true!” I fought back my smile. He stayed silent, grinning slightly. “I definitely won’t kiss you before you kiss me,” I said loudly before realizing that a senior couple was walking right behind us. As soon as I noticed them, I turned around and closed my eyes to hide the amount of shame that I was feeling right at that moment.

“You knew they were right behind us. Why didn’t you tell me?” I glared at Ayaan as the couple crossed the street and went in a separate direction after sheepishly smiling at me.

“And ruin my entertainment? How could I?” He took my hand in his again as we crossed the street to enter another market area.

“You’re mean!” I frowned.

“You’re cute.” He pinched my nose.

We kept walking until we found a shoe shop. Ayaan picked up simple red flip flops for me to try. They were really comfortable and fit me perfectly.

“Let’s go home?” he asked as he paid the cashier.

“Right now? You said you wanted to explore some more.” It was still quite early.

“I would rather explore something else,” he murmured in my ear as we walked out of the store. It took me a good minute to figure out what he meant…

“Ayaan?” I peeked up slowly and found his eyes on me.

“Do you want to go home?” he bit his lip, leaving me breathless for a moment. Now that we’ve confessed our feeling for each other...did it mean that we were ready to take a step forward and be intimate? I gulped. My throat got dry quickly.

“There’s still so much to see!” I looked down, letting the hair fall to cover my face. It was probably as red as a tomato.

“Whatever you say!” He nodded with a smile and continued walking, but I knew he was disappointed. I knew what he wanted, but I was so nervous. It would my first time. I loved Ayaan—I loved him endlessly—but I was feeling so shy. I didn’t know why I felt as if I were going to break the second he touched me.

“Are you upset?” I jogged after him.

“You know I could never be upset with you.” He glanced my way but didn’t hold my hand this time.

“I’m sorry…” I took his hand with my both hands to stop him.

“I can’t stay away from you. I just wanted today to be special...but I know I’m being selfish and I’m only thinking about myself. I don’t want to force you…” He didn’t look me in the eye when he said that. Was he feeling guilting for telling me what he wanted?

“No... Ayaan...I want…” I stopped abruptly and his eyes met mine. He stared at me and waited for me to finish what I was trying to say.

Ayaan was my husband, and I knew what I felt for him was real, but I didn’t know why was I pulling myself away from him. I wanted Ayaan and me to be close. So that was it, wasn’t it?

“I want...” Why was I stopping? The way he looked at me, awaiting an answer, felt as if millions of people were watching me.

“Do I have to say it?” I complained.

“Yes.”

“I want you.” I closed my eyes and clenched onto his shirt as I got closer to him.

“I don’t want to force you into…”

“I want you,” I interrupted and opened my eyes to look at him. He took my hand and unclenched my fist.

“Do you want to go?” He took a step forward toward me and pecked my forehead. I nodded, closing my eyes again under his embrace.

"I love you." He pulled my chin up to make me look at him.

"I love you," I repeated tenderly as Ayaan took my hand and led me to his car.

Chapter 27

Noor

It started raining as we approached the driveway. The dark clouds took over and everything turned gray.

"It's raining," I blustered at the fierce sound of the storm.

"You don't say!" Ayaan joked and I rolled my eyes. He was in a good mood and so was I, but I was also tense. I was still a bit anxious around Ayaan. The thought of being intimate with him made me feel nervous. He seemed calm and confident, whereas I was losing my mind and overthinking everything. Ayaan spoke his mind and carried his heart on his sleeve—he was the complete opposite from me. But strangely we clicked like two missing pieces of a puzzle.

"A penny for your thoughts..." he inquired as he unlocked the door of the car.

"I'll tell you once we get inside. Let's run for now." I smiled and ran toward the house to find shelter.

Ayaan jogged behind me, unlocked the door, and we entered our temporary residence. The heavy rain was hitting hard on the glass doors of the house, making me shiver. I enjoyed the rain, but sometimes it scared me. It had too much power. If out of control, it could bring chaos, and if in moderation, it could relieve the earth.

I turned to see Ayaan taking off his shoes. By the look on

his face, I could tell he wasn't a fan of the rain. It made me giggle, which made him look at me.

"What are you smiling about, missus?" He walked over to me and hooked his arm around my waist, pulling me closer to him.

"Ayaan, you're all wet!" I squealed.

"So are you." He flipped his hair back and continued holding me.

"We'll catch a cold," I murmured.

"I don't mind," he admitted in a flirty tone.

"You're unbelievable!" I couldn't help but smile.

"And you love that." He kissed my cheek, and when his lips left my skin, his nose brushed mine and my eyes fell on his lips. As soon as he noticed that, the smile on his face disappeared and his eyes got more intense, locking into mine. That look had the ability to shake my entire world. I tried to relax in his arms, but the emotion in his eyes kept me feeling jittery.

"Ayaan?"

"Noor." He waited, still not moving even an inch away from me. His eyes fixed to me, completely firm.

"Thank you." I blinked to keep my tears away. I never wanted to let him go.

"For what?" He brought his hand up to my face to keep me from looking down.

"For coming into my life. For allowing me to start a new life with you. For understanding me and trusting me and loving my parents as much—if not more than—you love yours. For teaching me how to love and be selfless and for encouraging me to believe in myself. I felt so lost after losing Mariam, but you made things better for me. Thank you for helping me move on. I love you, Ayaan." I took my hands that were resting on his chest and wrapped them around his waist, hugging him.

He picked me up in his arms and took me to our room, sitting me down on the bed first. He sat right next to me. He brought his cold fingers to my hand and I put my hand in his, responding to his touch. He looked at me intensely.

"Come here." He patted his lap, offering me a place to sit. I hesitated at first, but then I slowly moved toward him and did as I was told.

"You don't have to be nervous, Noor." He pushed my hair to the side. My neck was now completely exposed to him, and I could feel his breath on my bare skin. His fingers brushed down my back. Every single touch drove me crazy. I couldn't bear to look him in the eye.

"The only person in my heart now is you, Noor. I'm crazy about you," he whispered as his lips touched my neck. I held his shirt tightly.

"Look at me," he insisted, and my heart felt as if it had stopped for a minute. The anticipation rushed through me. I shifted my eyes toward him and noticed him already watching at me with intense need.

"You'll catch a cold," he repeated the same thing I said earlier. Before I could understand what he meant, he moved his hands away from my back and brought them forward to my collar. He undid the top two buttons of my shirt and returned his gaze to me, as if asking for permission. I felt a strange pounding in my chest and my breathing became uneven.

He was waiting, testing me as our heartbeats were now beating at a similar pace. I moved my hands from his shirt and circled them around his neck bringing him closer to me.

"So will you," I leaned closer to him and whispered in his ear slowly, allowing him to move forward.

"Damn it," I heard him say under his breath as he gently pulled my hair back and kissed me passionately, his other hand clenching my waist as he closed all the distance between us. His touch was consuming every part of my body, and I was losing myself in him.

"You're mine. Promise me you'll always be with me," he urged between kisses.

"I'm yours. I'll never leave you," I promised, as he pushed me down onto the bed, coming down on top of me.

Chapter 28

Noor

"Yes, Ammi, I packed everything. Okay, Ayaan is waiting outside. I'll call you from the airport. I can't wait to see you all. Bye now." I ended the call, grabbed my travel bag, and hurried outside.

The last moments with Ayaan here in Bulgaria were absolutely magical. I had never felt so much love and affection before. I actually felt like the luckiest girl in the world. We talked about our past, our fears, our dreams, our families and friends, our likes and dislikes, and everything in between. Every moment with him brought me closer to him, and him to me. We were not only in love, but also compatible. I knew that with him, no matter what happened, I would be okay.

"Here, let me get this." Ayaan approached me, taking the bag from my hand to putting it in the backseat of the taxi.

"Did you return the keys?" I asked him as I got inside the cab.

"Yes, everything is taken care of. You got everything?" He got inside and checked his phone. We were on schedule.

"Newly married, yeah?" our cab driver asked us. He looked to be in his late forties, half bald with a full-grown gray mustache.

"Yes, sir," Ayaan answered happily, still on his phone replying to work emails.

"You can do that when we get home. Put it away." I snatched his phone and put it in my bag. Ayaan was about to reach for it, but I glared at him and he pulled his hand away.

"Okay, boss." He shook his head pretending to be mad, but I could see a hint of a smile on him.

"You secretly like it when I boss you around, don't you?" I asked. He rolled his eyes and I laughed.

"You're blushing." I patted his cheek and moved my eyes from him to the driver. Ayaan knew I wasn't a fan of being too romantic in public.

"Noor..." He smirked and, in a swift motion, brought my face closer to his.

"Ayaan...don't. He can see us." I was in a flirty mood, but wanted to keep a distance. Ayaan had other plans.

"Who's blushing now?" He kept his hold sturdy on the back of my neck.

"You kids sure you want to go to the airport?" the cab driver jokingly said as he stopped the car at the red light. I looked away immediately, pushing Ayaan away from me.

"You sure, baby?" Ayaan called me baby. I never liked it when I heard people calling their partners cute pet names—I found them cheesy—but when Ayaan said it, it sounded too good. Perfect.

"Ayaan, please." I pleaded, asking for him to stop teasing me like that. His eyes were too addicting, too sweet, but also naughty. He let go of my neck, but grabbed my shoulder, keeping me close to him.

“Stay here, like this,” he proposed.

I rested my head on his shoulder giving in because, despite feeling strange sometimes in public when he flirted with me, being in his arms was now my favorite place in the whole world. I placed my hand on his chest and closed my eyes, feeling relaxed.

“Remember how you felt when your dad first brought this trip up over dinner?” he asked after a few moments of beautiful silence.

“Yes,” I remembered.

“You were so scared,” I heard him say softly.

“I was. But you seemed sure.”

“I was.” He nodded, and I lifted my head slightly to look at him.

“Why? What made you so sure about us?”

“You. Do you remember the night of the incident with the bikers? The moment I saw you in that dark alley, I was taken aback. The look on your face scared me. I didn’t know if there was anyone left in my life who would care so much if something were to happen to me. I knew you cared about me before, but that night, I knew something had changed between us. It wasn’t just an affection or sympathy that we felt for each other, it was beyond that...” The corners of his lips curled as he finished.

“It did. I’m glad you figured it out or we would have wasted a lot of time being separated from each other. I can’t even imagine being away from you now.” I lowered my head again and closed my eyes.

"Life is crazy. Let's just pray that however much time we get, we spend it together. But if a time comes where things change and it becomes too painful for you, for whatever reason, just know you can walk away, Noor."

His words broke my heart. I shot up to find him looking at me as if he were praying for me. I don't know why, but it brought tears to my eyes.

"Ayaan...why did you say that like that?" My eyes got watery, and I looked at him so he could explain himself.

"We're here," the cab driver announced, turning off the radio. Ayaan broke our eye contact.

After paying the cab driver and going inside, Ayaan kept most of his attention on other things. It was after we went through customs that I realized he was avoiding me. When we got to the gate, I knew he could tell that I still wanted to discuss what happened in the taxi.

"Ayaan..." I started.

"Do you want anything? Coffee? Right, you don't even drink coffee. I'll get some tea." He was about to get up when I stopped him.

"You're not going anywhere until you tell me what exactly happened in the taxi just now. Why did you say those things to me? Is something wrong?" I kept my hand on his.

"Forget what I said. It was stupid. I didn't know you were going to start crying. That's the last thing I wanted." He closed his eyes for a brief moment, still trying to avoid looking at me.

"Look at me," I insisted , and he finally listened.

"Say it...whatever it is. Spill it. What did it mean?"

Even the thought of us being apart didn't settle right with me. It suffocated me.

"I had a bad dream last night where I saw you crying, and someone was shouting at you. And then I saw that person: It was me. I was the one shouting at you, and you were shaking and crying, begging me to stop yelling," Ayaan told me as he clenched his hands tightly.

"It was just a dream. I've had terrible dreams, too, Ayaan," I tried consoling him.

"It felt real. It was so real. The fear in your eyes when you were talking to me...it scared me so much. I couldn't function after I woke up from that dream." He tightened his jaw.

"You should've woken me up, Ayaan. It was a dream. It didn't mean anything. I know you would never do that to me." I touched his cheek.

"I hated myself. I felt like I was actually doing that to you. Hurting you. I... Noor, I still mean what I said. I don't know what that dream meant, but all I know is that I love you and I always will, but if there's ever a time I turn into a type of a person who tortures you or humiliates you, walk away from me. No matter what. I can't describe how close to reality that dream felt, and that's why I'm telling you all of this." He carefully touched my cheek to wipe my tears.

The waiting area wasn't that busy, but even if it were, I wouldn't have cared. I wanted Ayaan to know that I was here for him. The things he said to me were too much for me to comprehend. I didn't know how to react, so I remained silent.

"Good afternoon, passengers. We're now inviting those passengers with small children, business-class passengers, and any passengers requiring special assistance to begin boarding at this time. Please have your boarding pass and identification ready. Regular boarding will begin in approximately ten minutes' time. Thank you."

The announcement broke our silence.

"Let's get going." Ayaan got up and offered his hand. I took it.

"I shouldn't have said all that. I'm such an idiot. Jeez. I'm sorry." He stopped walking and put his hand on my shoulders.

"You are an idiot, that's for sure." I shook my head. He gave a sad-looking smile in return.

"You can't say stuff like that to me. I'm not going to walk away from you, ever. I'm your wife and I love you, and you don't get to decide my future for me. I will stay with you forever, and I won't let you leave me, either. We can't be apart," I whispered.

"Yeah...it was just a bad dream," he sighed and nodded in my direction.

"Idiot." I entangled my arm with his and headed to board the plane. This time I finally managed to make him smile.

Chapter 29

Noor

"I'm so glad you guys went on this trip," Ammi said to me as she packed Hamza's clothes. After staying with them for two extra days, it was finally time to return to our home.

"Yes, me too. Ayaan and I are so thankful for you guys. This trip wouldn't have been possible if the two of you weren't here to look after him." I looked down at Hamza who was playing with my shirt.

"It wasn't just us. Huma also came several times to check in on him." She sat next to me and put Hamza's baby bag on the floor next to the bed.

"Yes, she loves him dearly." I kissed Hamza's cheeks and he giggled. He was such a playful baby, and I was starting to see his parents in him. He had Mariam's eyes, and his smile resembled Ayaan's.

"We're so proud of you. You're taking great care of this family. Without you, Ayaan and Hamza would be lost." My mother patted my shoulder.

"I guess all of us would be lost without each other. I wouldn't have found a guy like Ayaan even if I tried. He's a great man. He loves me, respects me, takes care of my needs. He's patient, loyal, honest, selfless, intelligent...I sometimes think he's not even real." I couldn't help but smile.

"I know, dear. You didn't have to tell me all this. The minute you guys walked in from your trip, I knew everything had worked out between the two of you. It's all in the eyes—they don't lie," she pointed out, and I blushed.

She was right, after coming back from the trip, Ayaan and I were inseparable.

Just then, Ayaan knocked on the door and poked his head in. He grinned as soon as he saw me and I smiled right back. My mother coughed in the back, so Ayaan cleared his throat and walked inside.

"Are you done packing?" he asked me.

"Ammi did it," I reported and followed him. Ayaan picked up Hamza and spun him around, and Hamza's giggles lit up the whole room.

"What would we do without you, Ammi?" He sat next to my mother and put his arm around her shoulder.

"That's what parents do for their kids. It's an eternal love, my son. You will do the same when Hamza grows up and has a child," she responded and Ayaan's smile grew.

The thought of Hamza getting married one day and having his own kids made me emotional. What a beautiful circle of life this was, a never-ending journey.

"Yes, but there's plenty of time for that." My father joined the conversation as he entered the room. "You sure you guys want to leave? You can stay for longer..."

"He just wants Hamza to be with him all the time now," my mother teased, and Ayaan and I laughed. It was true. Hamza had that effect on everyone. He was a happy kid.

Everyone always wanted to be around him, just like his father.

“Don’t worry, Baba, we’ll drop by soon. I have a lot of work to catch up on, but Noor can come here whenever she wishes,” Ayaan told them.

“No, we’ll come together,” I remarked.

“We’ll visit soon,” he added. “Let’s go. Huma’s at home, waiting.” Ayaan got up to leave. Ammi and Baba walked us outside, and we got into the car and drove home.

“My kids are home!” Huma’s greeted us as soon as our car entered the driveway. She was standing by the door, waiting for us outside.

I passed Hamza to Ayaan and ran to Huma to hug her. I missed her so much.

She kissed my head.

“You both were away for too long; this house was too quiet without you and my little prince.” She held my shoulders.

“What about me?” Ayaan came forward, and Huma touched his arm and took us inside. The house was just like we left it. It was clean, the daily newspaper was on the dining table, and there was a fresh bunch of flowers in the vase waiting for us.

“You managed the house so well, Huma,” I complimented her.

“You kids must be hungry. Should I heat up the food?” she offered.

“No, we already ate, but could you make us some tea?”

Ayaan asked.

"Tea? Since when have you started drinking tea?" she teased him and eyed me.

"Huma!" he chuckled, and I shook my head knowing she was doing that to tease us.

"Okay, fine, I'll stop messing with the two of you. Here, I'll take him, you guys go and change." She took Hamza from Ayaan, and we both went upstairs.

"It feels so nice to be back," I announced as I put the bag down on the bed and opened the closet to pick a clean set of pajamas for Ayaan and me.

"Yes, it does." Ayaan grabbed me from behind and rested his chin on my shoulder.

"Ayaan!" I squealed.

"Noor..."

"Huma is waiting for us and you're in the mood for romance?" I pretended to complain.

"I'm always in the mood to romance..." His lips hovered over my neck.

"Ayaan, seriously, leave me alone," I laughed and lightly hit his stomach with my elbow, but he didn't move. Instead, he held me tighter.

"Okay, I'll let you go, but there's one condition..." I could feel his lips curling upward.

"Let me guess, you want a kiss?" I turned my head and saw him smirking again. I was right.

"That's why I love you," he answered, looking down on me.

"You love me because I know when you want me to kiss me?"

"No, I love you because you always know what I'm thinking. It's like I don't even have to tell you, you just know." He brushed my hair away from my face.

"You're so demanding." I turned completely so that I could see him properly. I brought my hands around his neck to pull him closer to me. I missed being in his arms. The past two days in my parents' house I spent most of the time with them, and although Ayaan and I were together, we weren't alone together.

"You're so sexy." His hands traveled down my back, pulling me up. I rolled my eyes. "It's true. Everything about you is attractive. I like how you always have an opinion about everything and how you bite your lip when you're trying too hard to focus on something. I like the way you roll your eyes when you don't believe someone and the way you give yourself so selflessly for the people you love. I admire all of you." His voice was so warm and caring, but it was more than enough to drive me crazy and make my heart skip a beat.

"I've never seen anyone try so hard for a kiss," I joked, and he laughed generously.

"A man can dream." His dimple showed.

"Well if it makes you feel any better, the feelings are mutual." I tried not to smile, but failed.

"I'm glad to hear that." He brought his face closer to mine and his voice got lower. I kept backing away until my back hit the closet.

"No escaping now, wifey." And with that, his lips met

mine, and I couldn't be happier with his soppy gesture.

Chapter 30

Noor

"C'mon everyone's here. Are you ready?" My mother hurried inside my room as I was dressing Hamza.

"Yes, almost...just pass me his bowtie. It's on the dressing table," I rushed.

"Oh God, Noor, hurry...all the guests are waiting," my mother complained and went to pick up Hamza's bowtie. She handed it over to me and I clipped it on his shirt. She was in more of a hurry than anyone in the house.

"It's okay, Ammi. Baba and Ayaan are taking care of the guests. Here...now he's all ready. Look at him..." I smiled at Hamza. My little boy was a year old now. He was smiling back at me with so much love, as if I were a gift of some kind. But in reality, he was my gift.

"It's like he can understand what I'm saying." I glanced over at my mother, who was watching me with awe.

"Of course he understands, you're his mother." She patted my head.

"I miss Mariam." My eyes got teary remembering her.

"Don't be sad. Mariam isn't here with us, but she left a piece of herself in Hamza, and you'll always have that."

"Ready?" Ayaan walked in just then, smiling. He saw me and his beautiful smiled disappeared, worry taking over his face.

"Are you okay? What happened?" he asked my mother.

"Nothing. She just got a bit emotional. You know how she is... Don't take too long, the guests are waiting," she told us, leaving the room.

"You look handsome," I praised him. He was dressed in a beige t-shirt, navy blue blazer, and white trousers.

"And you're trying to change the subject." He half-smiled and sat next to me.

"I was thinking about Mariam," I told him, watching to see if he would react differently. It was almost as though he was expecting it. "You don't think about her?" I asked him and instantly regretted it. "I shouldn't have...forget it."

"I do think about her. It's natural. I think about her when Hamza reaches his milestones. Like last month, when he finally stood on his own and took his first step, I thought about her." He kept looking at me while he spoke.

"Things would have been different if..." I started.

"Don't," he interrupted. "Things turned out the way they were supposed to. You weren't my default, you're my choice. I was meant to be with you, and you with me, okay?" I touched his hand and nodded.

"I love you so much," I whispered.

"I live for you and Hamza." He kissed my forehead, then Hamza's made a noise and we both laughed. "Okay, okay I won't flirt with your mother," Ayaan joked and picked Hamza up. "Shall we?" Ayaan offered me his other hand and I gladly took it.

I didn't even recognize our living room. Huma, Ayaan, Ammi, Baba...everyone spent the entire morning decorating this place. It looked great.

"This looks amazing!" I squeezed Ayaan's hand as he walked us over to the table where a delicious-looking birthday cake was waiting for us. As soon as Hamza saw it, he started clapping. He looked so cute, and everyone started taking pictures.

"Okay, let's cut the cake, shall we?" Ayaan announced, and everyone gathered around the table.

Ayaan grabbed Hamza's hand and wrapped it around the knife, and I placed my hand on top of theirs. We all cut the cake together, and everyone began clapping and singing happy birthday. It was such a memorable moment, and everyone came to wish us well.

"I'll start cutting the cake for the guests," Huma offered.

"No, you're not working today. You've been working so much Huma...please."

"I won't listen to you. I'm doing it." She proceeded to cut the cake with a giant smile on her face.

"But..." I was about to go and stop her when Ayaan blocked me.

"Where are you going?" he asked.

"She's cutting the cake. I told her not to work. She's going to get wear herself out. Do you know she was up all night cleaning, even though I told her I'd call the cleaners this morning? And she wouldn't let me do anything today, either." I felt bad for her.

"It's her way of showing love for us and Hamza. Don't stop her; she won't listen."

"I can hear you two," Huma called from distance.

"I know you can. We love you!" I yelled back, and she grinned. I loved her as much as my own mother.

"Where's my prince?" Ayaan's mother walked toward us and took Hamza.

"Mama, you brought so many gifts! As did Noor's parents. You're all going to spoil him," Ayaan told his mother.

"He's our grandson. Of course, we're going to spoil him!" My father also joined us. Ayaan's mother shook her head in agreement.

"Noor!" I heard a familiar voice, and I looked out and saw my friend Somiya. I excused myself and went to go see her.

"Hey, you made it!" I hugged her.

"Of course! You know how Ali is...he's terrible with directions." She referred to her new husband. She got married a few months back.

"How's it going?" Ali greeted us.

"Assalam O Alikum, Ali," I welcomed him.

"Walikum Asalam. Sorry we're late!" He gave me a gift bag.

"Oh, that's okay, thank you. So when are you guys moving?" When I spoke to Somiya last, she told me they were moving to the US.

"Next month...his parents are eagerly waiting for us," she said shyly. What was she blushing about?

“Where’s Ayaan?” Ali asked and I pointed over to where he was standing. He excused himself and left us girls to chat.

“What are you blushing about?” I eyed her.

“I’m pregnant!” Her eyes glittered with excitement, as did mine. I was so happy for her.

“This is a wonderful news. I’m so happy for you! You both will be such wonderful parents.” I held her hands and gave them a tight squeeze.

“Thank you.” She was glowing.

“May you always stay happy.” I touched her cheek.

“Congratulations, Somiya!” Ayaan joined us with Ali and she blushed again.

“Thank you, Ayaan,” she smiled. Ayaan touched her head, giving her his blessings.

When it was time for them to leave, I said to Somiya, “Well, you better stay in touch!”

“Of course we will. We had such a great time. You’re a match made in heaven...and Hamza is such a sweet boy. Such a beautiful family. God bless you.” Somiya embraced me again, and they left moments later.

“Nice guy,” Ayaan said to me after we walked them out to their car.

“Yes.” I was about to go inside the house when he grabbed my elbow and pulled me closer to me.

“Ayaan...” I fake-glared at him.

“Noor...” he hummed and gave me a soft kiss on my

cheek.

"What was that for?" I asked playfully.

"I just wanted to look at you." He pushed my hair behind my ear and kept looking at me lovingly. I kissed his cheek in return. I felt beautiful and seen whenever he looked at me like that or took time to be with me. His love toward me only grew with time, and I was so thankful to have found someone so great who loved me without any conditions, and for whom the way I was, was simply enough.

"What was that for?" he smirked.

"You're my strength. Without you, I wouldn't have figured out what it meant to love someone so endlessly." I touched his face.

"And you're mine. If you weren't here, I would never have experienced all this happiness. You're a very important part of my life." He hugged me.

"Ayaan...Noor...where are you guys? Hamza just said his first word!" I heard my mother asking about us inside. We rushed in.

"What did he say?" I asked and followed my mother to where Hamza was. Hamza was sitting on Huma's lap and giggling.

"Oh, look who's here? Hamza, say the word now. Come on, say mama."

"He said mama?" I blinked. I couldn't believe it. Ayaan wrapped his arm around my shoulders. I was excited to see if he'd repeat it.

"Say it, my son. Say mama." I got on my knees and took Hamza in my arms. He was smiling brightly at me and said his first beautiful word again. I couldn't help myself from crying. I kissed both his cheeks and his forehead.

"Did you hear it? He said mama!" I turned to see Ayaan who had his phone out. He was recording it. He sat next to me and played the clip again for me to see. It was a miracle! My life, my love, my son, my family...they were all miracles from God. Humans weren't capable of creating such moments ourselves.

"Ayaan!" I was smiling but I was also crying because I was so indescribably happy. Right now, in that moment, I felt whole.

After everyone left, everything got quieter, but the sound of Hamza saying mama kept on ringing in my ears.

"Okay, I'm off to sleep now. Hamza finally fell asleep." Huma walked out of the room into the living room where I was cleaning up.

"Thank you, Huma...for everything. You take such good care of us," I thanked her.

"There's no need to thank me. Seeing you all happy fills my heart." She was about to start helping me with the cleaning, but I stopped her.

"No, I got this...you go sleep. Please." I took the plates from her hands.

"No, this is a lot. How are you going to clean all this?" She tried to take the plates from me again.

"I will help her; you go and sleep," Ayaan voice came from the stairs. He came to us and put his hand on her shoulder.

"Okay...help her clean. Don't let her do all the work." She

told him and he nodded. They had such a great bond. It was lovely to see their connection flourish over time.

"Okay, teacher," he teased her, and she left the room laughing.

"Let me." He took the plates from my hand and started cleaning. He helped me with the washing, he wiped the tables, and cleaned the stove. He never complained, not even once.

"You must be tired. Go and get some rest," I told him, but he ignored me and continued on working.

"Ayaan…" I went up to him and tapped on his shoulder. "Go and get some rest. I'll do this." I tried to take the cleaning cloth from his hand, but instead he used his free hand and pulled me closer to him.

"We'll rest together." His eyes look tired, but he was still smiling.

"You look so tired." I pushed his hair back.

"So do you, but you're still working, so why can't I do the same?"

"You have work tomorrow. You have to wake up early."

"And what about you? You also wake up countless times through the night to check on Hamza and then you wake up to cook for me before I leave for work. You do just as work as me, if not more." The way he complimented me, even in the smallest way, made me fall in love with him even deeper.

"How did I get so lucky? I hope our son turns out like you." I stared up at him.

"Charming, handsome, and intelligent?" He bit his lip.

"Yes, and kind, respectful, caring, compassionate, loving, patient, sensitive, hard-working, and encouraging."

"That's a long list."

"It's all true." I wrapped my arms around him and rested my head on his chest.

"I hope he turns out like you." He rested his chin on my head.

"Like me?" I asked and he nodded.

"I hope he grows up to be loyal, understanding, kind-hearted, a little playful, smart, sincere, empathetic, and responsible" he continued, and I moved my head up to look at him.

As we looked at each other I couldn't help but think about our past: we got married, we shared each other's pain and happiness, we fell in love and created this life with our son.

"We have come a long way, haven't we?" I lowered my eyes.

"We have, and we have a long way to go, don't we?"

"All those bad dreams... that was all fear, a lie. I've never been happier." I sighed, feeling a great sense of gratitude toward the life and love that I was blessed with.

"You're right," he agreed, holding me lovingly in his arms.

"I'll always keep falling in love with you," I confessed.

"I'll never stop loving you."

He pulled my chin up and kissed me like he'd been waiting to do it for hours. Ayaan was my soulmate, my best friend, my lover, and the father of our beautiful child. I was in love with each and every one of his roles. He came into my life when I was shattered, and he somehow managed to revive me. He challenged me, adored me, fought for me, loved my flaws, gave me hope, taught me how to live a happy life, and never left my side. He took away the thorns and turned my life into an amazingly happy one.

Ayaan and me? We were a forever kind of a thing now.

Thank you for reading!

www.ingramcontent.com/pod-product-compliance
Ingram Content Group UK Ltd.
Pitfield, Milton Keynes, MK11 3LW, UK
UKHW041837190726
13854UKWH00002B/576

9 781777 378004